PAINTING
THE FUTURE

ALSO BY LOUISE L. HAY

BOOKS

Colors & Numbers
Empowering Women
Everyday Positive Thinking
Experience Your Good Now! (book-with-CD)
A Garden of Thoughts: My Affirmation Journal
Gratitude: A Way of Life (Louise & Friends)
Heal Your Body
Heal Your Body A–Z
Heart Thoughts (also available in a gift edition)
I Can Do It® (book-with-CD)
Inner Wisdom
Letters to Louise
Life! Reflections on Your Journey
Love Your Body
Love Yourself, Heal Your Life Workbook
Meditations to Heal Your Life (also available in a gift edition)
Modern-Day Miracles
The Power Is Within You
Power Thoughts
The Present Moment
The Times of Our Lives (Louise & Friends)
You Can Create an Exceptional Life (with Cheryl Richardson)
You Can Heal Your Life (also available in a gift edition)
You Can Heal Your Life Companion Book

BOOKS FOR CHILDREN

The Adventures of Lulu
I Think, I Am! (with Kristina Tracy)
Lulu and the Ant: A Message of Love
Lulu and the Dark: Conquering Fears
Lulu and Willy the Duck: Learning Mirror Work

and

THE LOUISE L. HAY BOOK COLLECTION
(comprising the gift versions of *Meditations to Heal Your Life, You
Can Heal Your Life,* and *You Can Heal Your Life Companion Book*)

All of the above are available at your
local bookstore, or may be ordered by visiting:

Hay House USA: **www.hayhouse.com®**; Hay House Australia:
www.hayhouse.com.au; Hay House UK: **www.hayhouse
.co.uk;** Hay House South Africa: **www.hayhouse.co.za;**
Hay House India: **www.hayhouse.co.in**

Louise's Websites: **www.LouiseHay.com®**
and **www.HealYourLife.com®**

PAINTING
THE FUTURE

A *Tales of Everyday Magic* Novel

LOUISE L. HAY

and Lynn Lauber

Based on a screenplay by
Ron Marasco and Brian Shuff

VISIONS

HAY HOUSE, INC.

Carlsbad, California • New York City
London • Sydney • Johannesburg
Vancouver • Hong Kong • New Delhi

Published and distributed in the United States by: Hay House, Inc.: www.hayhouse.com® • *Published and distributed in Australia by:* Hay House Australia Pty. Ltd.: www.hayhouse .com.au • *Published and distributed in the United Kingdom by:* Hay House UK, Ltd.: www.hayhouse.co.uk • *Published and distributed in the Republic of South Africa by:* Hay House SA (Pty), Ltd.: www.hayhouse.co.za • *Distributed in Canada by:* Raincoast: www.raincoast.com • *Published in India by:* Hay House Publishers India: www.hayhouse.co.in

Cover design: Mario San Miguel • *Interior design:* Tricia Breidenthal

Library of Congress Control Number: 2011937385

Tradepaper ISBN: 978-1-4019-3781-2
Digital ISBN: 978-1-4019-3782-9

15 14 13 12   4 3 2 1
1st edition, January 2012

Printed in the United States of America

CHAPTER 1

This is a story of love and hope—and how two strangers saved each other at what seemed like the last possible moment.

✧ ✧

It was another scorching July morning in San Francisco's Mission District, a neighborhood where everything green and lovely had seemingly disappeared. The sweet chestnuts and peppermint willows of the past were gone, and the lawns paved over with asphalt black as licorice.

Lupe, roller-skating in an apartment courtyard, seemed the exception. There was something fresh and new about her. At 11, she was loose limbed, with long dark hair drawn back in a ponytail. In certain light, she had a timeless beauty older than her years—the look of a saint in an Italian fresco.

But when she smiled, her face revealed an impish dimpled grin—and she was a girl again.

Weaving around the circular driveway of the courtyard, she sang a song under her breath. *"The use of love makes me feel good. It is an expression of my inner joy."*

She stopped to admire an old-fashioned rose that had twined around a chain-link fence to produce a burst of apricot-colored flowers.

She looked up to a second-floor apartment window, where, as if by magic, an elderly woman's face appeared, brown as a nut and deeply lined.

"Grandma, look!"

"Sí, sí. ¡Muy bonita! Watch out for thorns," the old woman called, but her words were lost in a splash of salsa music that had been turned up inside.

Lupe would not have heeded her anyway; she focused only on beauty.

This did not bother Juana Saldana—it was what she had taught her granddaughter. It was how they all survived.

The grandmother turned back into their second-floor apartment, filled with moving boxes and the sound of persistent pounding. The apartment was shabby, with old appliances and worn carpets. An older man silently wandered in with a large potted plant and placed it in the living room, then retreated again.

The hammering was soon joined by another sound, a buzzing in the apartment next door, 206.

A harsh male voice called out over the din, "I hear you, I hear you!" and pushed an intercom in response.

The door swung open to reveal the long, furious face of a tall man in his 50s—Jonathan Page. With flowing salt-and-pepper hair, he looked both distinguished and dissipated, a prince who had fallen on hard times. His face was slender, with high cheekbones and generous lips. He was wearing an expensive linen shirt stained with tomato sauce, and wire-rim glasses with dark lenses. In his right hand he gripped a fistful of dollars.

He peered out his window into the courtyard. "Are you in yet?" he called.

The intercom continued buzzing.

"I buzzed you in already, for God's sake!"

He stormed back to the intercom and pushed it again.

The voice of a deliveryman blasted out. "Yo! I've got a delivery for—"

Jonathan interrupted; he was unaccountably angry. Everything seemed to make him furious these days. Just this week he'd blown up at the meter reader, the Chinese-food deliveryman, and the man who cut his hair once a month. Why? Because he hated being stuck in his crummy apartment, reliant on others.

"Yo, yourself. I'm buzzing you in one more time. When you hear it, open the door. It's that large metal object right in front of your face."

He cursed as he hit the buzzer again. The deliveryman finally opened the door and entered.

Lupe stopped skating and stood in the courtyard, watching with fascination as Jonathan poked his head in and out of the window.

The persistent pounding coming from the apartment next door grew even louder.

"Will you stop that racket?" Jonathan yelled, dropping some of his money on the floor. "Goddamn it!" He got down on his hands and knees and felt around.

The deliveryman reached the top of the landing and found Page searching the floor.

"I got a package for Mr. Page."

"I know my name, thank you very much," Page said, still groping around the floor until he found the last dollar. He struggled up and handed the money to the deliveryman. "Here—it's exact."

Below them was the sound of skating. Lupe, who had entered the lobby, now stood at the bottom of the stairs, looking up.

"And there's no skating in this building!" Page called down. "Go skate in the street, why don't you? It's more dangerous."

As the deliveryman took the money and followed him into the apartment, he finally got a look at Page's face. "Hey—oh, damn, man, I didn't realize. You blind."

Jonathan scowled and turned away. "Put that package on the table, and pick up the other one. It's ready to be sent. And be careful."

"*Yo.* I know my job."

"*Yo* isn't a word," Page said primly and walked away.

As the deliveryman turned to leave, he muttered, "Well, *prick* is."

The deliveryman thundered down the stairs and encountered Lupe as he left. He gave her a look of exasperation and camaraderie.

"Man, what a monster."

"He's just confused."

"You know him?"

"No," she said, and hesitated. "Not yet."

◇ ◇

Lupe was living with her grandparents, but she often thought about her parents, who'd moved back to Mexico. In the last year, they'd both lost their jobs in the States: her father in construction, her mother as a housekeeper in a nursing home. Since they were undocumented, they couldn't receive unemployment, and no matter how they tried, they were unable to find other work.

Lupe had watched as they came home each evening, avoiding her eye, and talked in hushed, worried tones. She noticed how they counted the worn dollars they stashed at the bottom of her mother's drawer. She had seen her father's normally cheerful face grow gaunt and lined, noticed that her mother had found new ways to prepare rice and beans every night.

These last months, when the bottom had fallen out of their lives, the family had had to make a hard choice about who would go and who would stay in America. In the end, it was decided that Lupe would remain with her grandparents, and her parents would return. Lupe remembered—with a pang—that terrible conversation, when her mother had called her into the living room with her special, formal voice.

"Daddy and I are going back. That's the way it has to be for now."

When Lupe had cried, her mother took her into her arms. "It won't be forever, mi amor," she said, fighting her own tears. "It's for the best, you understand."

The fact that the move was a financial necessity didn't make it any easier.

Lupe missed having her father sit with her as she studied her history lessons and help her with math; she missed her mother's laugh in the morning and the way her smile brightened the day.

She even missed Axochiapan, the Mexican village she was from, which was lush, beautiful, and extremely poor. When her parents had lived with her, she'd rarely thought about their village; but now that they were so far away, she dreamed about the bougainvillea, the nearby lagoon, and the warm feeling that overcame her when neighbors mingled together in backyards after dinner to cool off from the day. She remembered how her best friend, Maria, would come over, and they'd play in the dusty backyard. Lupe would always be the teacher or the nurse, and Maria would be the student or patient. They both planned on having careers when they grew up, unlike their mothers. They dreamed about going to college, having their own bikes, and being able to go to the grocery store on their own to pick out whatever items they desired.

Lupe yearned to at least visit her parents and friends, but her grandmother told her it wasn't possible. There was no money for such an extravagance. Plus, what if they didn't allow Lupe back into the country?

Her grandmother reminded her that Poppy's heart couldn't stand much more upheaval and unhappiness. But Lupe didn't have to be reminded of that.

She loved her grandfather, with his worn face, bleary eyes, and snaillike gait. Raul Saldana had once been vital and strong, a man who built homes and cut down trees. Lupe didn't remember this time—before emphysema and heart disease took away his strength—but there were photos strewn around the apartment that proved it. They also showed her grandmother in another incarnation, when she was a dark-eyed beauty who wore camellias in her hair. They posed in fancy clothes—her grandfather in a wide-brimmed hat and embroidered shirt, her grandmother in a wide-skirted dress with ruffles and flounces. They looked like the most vital people in the world, as if they would be young forever. For Lupe, these people lived right alongside the ancient people her grandparents had become. She could almost see them some nights, superimposed on their weary counterparts in the dim glow of the television.

CHAPTER 2

When Jonathan felt a breeze from the stairwell, he realized that the deliveryman had failed to shut his door, and he stalked over to slam it. On the way, he ran into the pungent lime aftershave that announced the presence of Mr. Antunucci, the landlord. Since he'd become blind, Jonathan had discovered that each person had a distinctive scent that preceded and surrounded him, like an aura; sometimes subtle colors also appeared in his mind. He had never told anyone this. Mr. Antunucci possessed not only a citrus scent but a rosy cloud.

"What's all the racket next door?"

"Hello, Mr. Page," Antunucci said in a voice that suggested he'd long been the recipient of Mr. Page's complaints. "I'm putting railings on the tub in here."

"Why do the Lees need railings?"

"The Lees moved out last month; an elderly couple's subletting now. The Saldanas."

"They must be plenty old if they need railings."

"You'll be old one day, too."

Jonathan muttered, "I doubt it."

"They're just renting for a couple of months. One of them is getting treatments across the street at the hospital."

"That dump? Tell them they'll pick up a nice case of staph."

"Try to be friendly."

An old man, slowly pulling an oxygen cart, emerged from the bedroom and made his way into the hall.

"Morning, Mr. Saldana," Antunucci said.

"Morning," the old man managed, then exploded into a long, phlegmy cough. Behind him in the apartment, salsa music was turned up.

Jonathan shook his head as he moved back into his apartment. "God help me."

Antunucci muttered, "You need it."

Lupe, who had been lurking just inside the Saldanas's apartment, skated out and peered at the name tag on Jonathan's door.

"That's Jonathan Page, the unhappiest man in the world," Mr. Antunucci said.

◇   ◇

Jonathan hadn't always been a fractious blind man, railing at neighbors and deliverymen. There was a time when he was the talk of the town, a

10

successful artist, part of a coterie of attractive, chic young men. He'd had shows in New York and Los Angeles and the capitals of Europe. His photograph seemed always to be in *The New York Times* Style section—smiling at this party or that opening, always dapper and handsome, always in the front row. He'd been profiled in the *LA Times* and the *Chicago Tribune;* he was so used to being interviewed on television that, in the end, it didn't even make him nervous anymore.

The prints and reproductions of his most famous painting, *The Dancing Vagabond,* had made him wealthy and famous. He'd tried not to be seduced by the attention and accolades, but it got under his skin. He became used to it, then he felt like he deserved it. He spent the money as quickly as he earned it. He bought a silver Jaguar and an apartment on Madison Avenue, dove-gray cashmere sweaters, and fur-lined coats.

He was estranged from his parents and sister—there had been words between them that could never be taken back. He had no other close relatives, so he had formed a family of his friends and fellow artists. They'd had Thanksgivings in Aspen and Christmases in the Caribbean; they'd flown to Hawaii so often that Jonathan finally bought a house in Maui, right on the beach, one of three he owned at the height of his wealth and power.

All this, he had assumed, would continue forever. His old money would make new money; his holdings would increase, as would his friendships.

His looks could always be augmented by a little nip and tuck.

But then, one fateful year, it all began to change.

Eventually, everything collapsed.

His friends got sick and then died one after another from a virus that no one was able to name or understand.

It seemed that as fast as Jonathan could paint his friends—those handsome young men with sculpted cheeks and thick pale hair—they grew wan and ghostlike. They entered hospitals and never emerged again. Instead of parties, he went to funeral homes, ghastly places that smelled of lilies. He stood in the back and watched families from other places—Kentucky and Mississippi— approach their lost sons with wails that would break the hearts of the most hardened people. These were the artistic boys who'd left home to become singers and actors. Now they were gone and so was the life that Jonathan had thought would always last.

Then Jonathan himself was stricken with a degenerative disease that stole his eyesight within a matter of months. First, he couldn't read newspapers; then it was the menus at restaurants. Next, he found himself avoiding painting, not because he didn't have ideas, but because he had difficulty making out his own lines. When his agent realized that he wasn't able to produce anymore, all the attention stopped as word swept the art world.

He was blind! Worse than dead, in his opinion, especially for a visual artist. He was reduced to an invisible, handicapped status. Overnight, he became a lonely man in rented rooms who needed assistance with nearly every aspect of his life.

The bitterness that had begun flooding Jonathan during that dying season never retreated. Ever since, his mouth had felt full of acrid bile. Everything bothered him. Unsolicited phone calls, TV advertisements, how hard it was to open a bottle of pills. Some nights in bed he had to will himself to remember that he'd ever had another life, since there were so few witnesses to that time.

How had he ended up here, in this noisy third-rate building, populated with illegal aliens and drug lords? He thought of what his friends would say if they could see him now, reduced to paying deliverymen to bring cheap Chinese meals.

He could barely get himself to leave the apartment anymore, except to sit on the chair outside his door and smoke his little imported cigars—one of his few remaining pleasures.

His daily life had been reduced to bed, bathroom, chair, and daily cigar. *What's the point of living like this?* he asked himself.

And what worried him most was that he no longer had an adequate answer.

✧   ✧

Lupe thought it was lucky that she loved old people, since they were the ones with whom she spent most of her time now. Her grandparents were her most constant companions. She played hearts with her grandfather after dinner and listened to her grandmother's stories late into the night.

She knew them all. There was the story of how her grandparents met on a blind date at a village dance. Her grandfather had walked in, dusty from a long day of road work, and her grandmother wouldn't speak to him until he went home, changed his clothes, and washed his hair.

There was the story about how Lupe's mother had been born breech, and her labor had taken all one day and night, nearly wearing out her grandmother, who called for the priest and begged to be taken to heaven. There were stories of husbands who strayed but returned home again; when they didn't, they underwent terrible punishments (from God, her grandmother said), losing a leg or a fortune or going bald overnight. Lupe couldn't get enough of these stories and their plots full of conflict and honor. The good always triumphed, eventually, in her grandmother's stories. None of them ever died, except for off-screen, post-story. Lupe liked being left with the uplifting moral. It made her feel better, as her grandmother knew it would.

Her grandparents' friends were *her* friends— old maroon-haired Mrs. Gonzalez who tapped over on two canes from apartment 102 to bring them fresh tortillas and neighborhood gossip; Mr. Santana from 109, who had recently lost his wife and came over at breakfast to silently weep into his café con leche. That was the hour he missed her most, he said. Her grandparents had an open-door policy, and Lupe was often the one who escorted in these seniors. She loved their frank manner and wrinkled faces and the way they told the truth.

But that didn't mean she didn't pine for friends her own age. Especially in school, where she hadn't yet found a group that would include her.

The Hispanic girls in her school seemed older than Lupe, who still kept a stuffed animal in her locker and had yet to wear a bra. These girls treated her with contempt when they noticed her at all.

"Lupe's still a baby. Aren't you, Lupe?" asked one of the sassiest, a girl named Rita, when Lupe walked by the group as they stood, snapping gum in the hall.

"No," Lupe said simply and tried to get past them as quickly as possible, so they wouldn't notice her frayed dress, washed and ironed by her grandmother, but still with a small hole in the back, or her out-of-style shoes, bought from the thrift store.

But Lupe was fascinated by the proud, pale-haired girls who predominated at her school, wealthy daughters of the town's doctors and dentists, who looked like princesses to her.

These girls had equally beautiful mothers who drove their SUVs right up to the curb, releasing their daughters in clouds of perfumed entitlement. One, named Brie, was so ethereal, so self-assured and beautiful, that Lupe couldn't help imagining being her friend. Brie was the epitome of social success; in the cafeteria, girls saved a spot for her at the head of a special table. She set the style for the year's cool clothes—this year it was short black ruffled skirts and tight midriff-clinging T-shirts—as well as the movies, books, and television shows that were favored. She never looked tired or discouraged. Her oval face was always slightly blushing, and her blue eyes were accented with just enough makeup. Lupe had never seen Brie break out in embarrassing rashes, as she herself sometimes did.

One afternoon Lupe gathered her courage and said to Brie, "I love the color of your shirt." It was a pale blue that reminded Lupe of the sky over her village in Mexico. But Brie looked at her as if she had just said the stupidest thing in the world.

Lupe was humiliated, but she managed not to burst out crying.

She just remembered her grandmother's advice about adversity and the power of positive thinking, and she adjusted her face and smiled at Brie in spite of the girl's dark and skeptical look.

"What is she *smiling* at?" Brie asked a friend who was standing next to her, and the two of them laughed as they sashayed off together.

CHAPTER 3

After school one day, Lupe coasted downhill on her bike, the wind fanning her hair out behind her. It was broiling hot and humid with the temperature in the high 90s, but Lupe hummed a song that the wind snatched away.

She stopped her bike in front of a squat brick building that housed one of the local libraries. She entered the computer room, sat down in front of a monitor, and typed in Jonathan's name. She couldn't believe it when a younger version of his face flashed on screen. It was him, but a happier-looking, darker-haired version, with a fuller face and laughter crinkling his eyes. There were pages of material about his art and life. Lupe read it all, spellbound.

"Celebrated as a painter, Jonathan Page is also a master printmaker, who has, over the course of more than 20 years, pushed the boundaries of traditional printmaking in extraordinary ways.

"Renowned for his saturated colors, bold style, and realistic depictions, Page's most famous painting, *The Dancing Vagabond,* has remained a best-selling print since it first appeared."

Lupe clicked onto the image of the painting. It showed a man standing on a lonesome street corner at night. He was long limbed like Jonathan and had his angular face and generous mouth. The man raised one arm in the air in a dancer's gesture. The painting was beautiful and evocative.

Lupe kept clicking and reading. "Tragically, Page's prodigious production was interrupted by a degenerative illness that struck in his 40s. Now completely blind . . . living somewhere in the San Francisco Bay Area . . . he has produced no new art since the onset of his illness."

Someone pointedly coughed behind her, and Lupe turned to find Brie with a supremely impatient look on her face. She was wearing her black skirt and tight top today, along with ropes of shiny necklaces. "Would you mind telling me how much longer you're going to be? I've got a paper due for social studies."

Lupe looked around; all the computers were occupied by people who had already been working when she arrived. Why didn't Brie approach them? But she shook her head to dislodge the thought and smiled at Brie instead.

"I'll finish up—I'm almost done. Sorry you had to wait."

She printed the article about Jonathan and then hastily gathered her books so Brie could take her place. Brie did so without a thank-you or a second glance.

Lupe hesitated a moment as if still expecting some word, but all Brie offered was a flip of her long golden hair. Standing behind her, Lupe watched as Brie signed onto Facebook.

Brie saw Lupe watching and gave her a tight little smirk.

⋄ ⋄

When Lupe arrived at home, she found Jonathan sitting in a straight chair outside his doorway, smoking a small cigar.

"Who's there?"

Lupe didn't speak for a moment, studying him, as if comparing him with the painting she'd looked at earlier in the day.

"You shouldn't smoke," she said.

"Who says?"

"Lupe."

"Well, Lupe, mind your own business," he said, blowing a dark ring directly toward her face.

"The air belongs to everyone," Lupe said.

"Oh, spare me. What are you doing here anyway? Do you live here? I think I've noticed you before. Do you wear perfume that smells like roses?"

"No!" said Lupe, as if this were an affront. "I don't wear perfume at all."

"Maybe it's shampoo. Or maybe it's just you." He didn't say that he also saw a silver-tinted light when he discerned this scent in the air.

"I'm staying with my grandparents," Lupe informed him. "They live next door."

Jonathan inhaled deeply. "Well, that must be fascinating. Are you training to be a nurse?"

"A nurse?"

"Never mind." He tapped his cigar on an ashtray. "By the way, whatever crap your grandmother fried last night smelled up my apartment all evening."

Under her breath, Lupe sang a little tune.

"What's that?"

"My grandmother says I should sing that whenever anyone swears."

Jonathan barked a laugh. "*Crap* is hardly a swearword. If you want to hear swearwords—"

Lupe quickly sang the ditty again.

"Stop it!" Jonathan said.

"What kind of nasty cigar is that, anyway?"

"It's an expensive kind, that's what."

"Please stop. My grandfather can barely breathe as it is."

"That's his problem."

"But your smoking will damage our friendship."

"Friendship?" He laughed. "How old are you, anyhow?"

"Eleven."

"Well, you're a little young for me, dear."

"How old are you?"

"Two hundred and twelve."

"Well, that's too old to be smoking. But since we're friends, I'll help you."

Lupe calmly removed the cigar from Jonathan's hand and began walking down the stairs.

"Hey! What are you doing? Give me that!"

He reached around, snatching at air. "I'm blind—I can't see you."

"I know," Lupe said, still descending.

"You little brat! Give that back!"

"It's okay; you can yell all you want. We'll still be friends. I've envisioned good things for you."

"What are you talking about?"

"Say good-bye nasty cigar."

"You little shit, what are you talking about?"

But Lupe was downstairs, singing under her breath and taking the cigar far into the alley, where she crushed it under her heel.

✧   ✧

Lupe's grandmother was her special confidante and adviser, the one who guided and inspired her. She had advice for every one of life's problems, most of it with a pointed personal story attached.

When a girl at school called Lupe a name, her grandmother told a story of a boy who had been called names and grew up to become a successful lawyer, able to fight for defendants who couldn't stand up for themselves.

Once when Lupe got into a fight because a boy tried to steal her purse, her grandmother taught her a wrist-twisting technique that made him drop her purse next time with a yelp of pain and surprise. "You can also use it if you want to get away fast," her grandmother said.

There was evidently nothing anyone had ever experienced that her grandmother didn't know about.

She taught Lupe songs to sing whenever she encountered negativity, a force that she spoke of as powerful and contagious, one that must be combated immediately, before it had the chance to seep into one's soul. Lupe's favorite began:

Deep at the center of my being, there is
an infinite well of love.
I now allow this love to flow to the surface.
It fills my heart, my body, my mind, my
consciousness, my very being, and radiates out from
me in all directions and returns to me multiplied.
The more love I use and give, the more I have to give;
the supply is endless.

Lupe had sung this so many times that she knew it by heart.

"Remember, there is an eye in your mind, and when you use it to see what you want, you bring it into your life," Lupe's grandmother taught her. "The words you use have strong power. Never use negative or swearwords, only positive words full of light."

"Spanish or English words?" Lupe asked.

Her grandmother laughed and put her arms around her. "It doesn't matter, my little petunia. Any words. Just make sure they are positive in your mouth and in your mind. See your life the way you want it to be; see the lives of those you love full of blessing and light. This is the secret of life . . . something everyone knows, but most everyone forgets."

Her grandmother's hug smelled like sweat and talcum powder. Whenever Lupe got scared at night, she wrapped her arms around her grandmother's neck and squeezed her tight.

CHAPTER 4

Another hot, oppressive day.

Lupe sat under an umbrella with a pitcher of lemonade, under a sign that read BEST LEMONADE IN TOWN. She had driven her bike all the way to Shop Town, even though her grandmother said that they overcharged poor people. She bought lemons, a pound bag of sugar, and filtered water. She stood in the kitchen while her grandmother gave her advice on how to make the best lemonade.

"Back home we drink *agua de limón* room temperature, but in America, people like everything cold. You have to add plenty of ice cubes and keep adding them, or no one will buy."

After a half hour, Lupe sat with only a few quarters in the jar beside her.

She smiled as a businessman, scowling into a cell phone, rushed by; he didn't even look her way. Nor did those who followed—a teenage jogger, a woman wearing a Bluetooth headset who seemed to be arguing with herself, a middle-aged woman in a tight white dress.

An SUV full of high-school boys stopped nearby at a light, and one of them looked over at Lupe derisively.

"Hey, *chiquita!*" someone called out, as if it were a curse.

The sun shifted; the day stretched on. Lupe's grandmother looked at her from the upper window—she seemed ready to call down, but then stopped herself.

A square of sweat formed on Lupe's forehead and ran in rivulets down the side of her face, but still she smiled. Another sign, flat on the table, with her arm covering it, read FOR A GOOD CAUSE.

Lupe closed her eyes and murmured, *"I only attract loving people in my world, for they are a mirror of what I am."*

She opened her eyes wide and looked around; now the sidewalk was completely empty except for a black dog who stopped for a moment to smell her shoe and then listlessly moved on.

Then, just as Lupe was thinking of giving up for the day, customers started arriving. A large family, stuffed in a hot car, stopped and ordered a glass each.

"Our air conditioner just went on the fritz," the father said.

Several boys pulled up on their bikes, as well as an assortment of children who wandered up, hot and thirsty, to empty their pockets of nickels and dimes.

By the time Lupe ran out of lemonade, the sun was low in the sky, and her jar was nearly full.

◇ ◇

Lupe climbed the stairs to the second-floor landing, with her disassembled stand to find Jonathan. He sat outside his door, almost finished with another cigar.

"Hi again, Mr. Jonathan."

He jumped. "God, don't sneak up on me like that." He pulled his cigar close to his chest. "And don't think about taking this away."

"I won't."

"I'm done anyhow." He stubbed it out in a planter.

"See? You quit, just like I said."

"I didn't quit, you little—" He stopped himself before Lupe could respond. "And I don't want to hear that stupid song again."

"So you're swearing less, too!"

"You're a pest, you know that? And a menace. I'm going to inform your grandparents. What are their names again?"

"Juana and Raul Saldana. *S-A-L-D-A-N-A.*"

"What an awful name. Too many *A*'s."

Lupe ignored him and pulled out a bag of coins. "I just finished selling lemonade. I made $28.25."

"From lemonade?"

"Well, from tips, too." She moved closer to him, as if to share a secret. "I need money for something very special. My *quinceañera*."

Jonathan made a face. "What's that? Some of your smelly food?"

"It's a big celebration, when I'm 15, that means I'm a woman. A band serenades you and everything, and I get to wear a gown and carry a bouquet of flowers."

"I thought you said you were only 11."

"I am, but I'm almost 12. And I have to start saving right now, so I can have the prettiest dress. I do extra jobs. Maybe I can work for you."

"Doing what? Annoying me? But you already do that for free."

"Seriously," Lupe said, with a grave look, "you need help."

Jonathan winced as if these words had pierced him.

"Some blind people have dogs," she said.

"You want to be my seeing-eye dog?"

"No, your seeing-eye Lupe."

"I don't need you."

"I already helped. I changed your lightbulb this morning, and I brought in a package that was sitting outside, and yesterday I brought in your mail and newspaper."

Jonathan replied, "Well, I didn't ask you to do any of that."

"I know. I wanted to." She went to her apartment door and opened it. "I want to see you happy." She shut the door.

Jonathan remained in his chair. "Happy?" He shook his head, and a look of pain crossed his face.

✧ ✧

Lupe had interrupted one of Jonathan's reveries, the reliving of a trip he and his partner, Georgie, had taken to Venice for Georgie's 25th birthday. It was a golden trip, one of their first together, when he had the distinct pleasure of introducing Georgie, a boy from Indiana, to a place that he considered one of the wonders of the world. They studied the art at the Doges Palace, drank wine in St. Mark's Square, and read from *The Merchant of Venice* as they slipped along quiet canals in a gondola.

Jonathan thought Georgie might faint when he first saw the Grand Canal.

"Do you know how ancient this is?" Georgie asked, his face rosy with excitement and his tawny hair flopped into his eyes.

Born in the Midwest, he had never traveled anywhere besides California. Jonathan had taught him everything he knew, schooling him on how to choose wine for dinner, how to pronounce *Rilke,* and what Chopin sounded like compared to Mozart. It was gratifying, the way Georgie appreciated it all.

"I wouldn't know anything without you!" he often said, turning to Jonathan adoringly with his pale eyes full of respect and love.

Really, he was the most adorable young man Jonathan had ever seen. Sometimes he could not believe his good luck.

Still, it was on that trip that Jonathan had the fleeting sense that this relationship couldn't possibly endure forever. Twenty years his junior, wouldn't Georgie eventually get bored and find someone younger, more handsome? The thought that Georgie might die before him had never entered his mind; still, the pessimistic side of him was always half waiting for the other shoe to drop.

This was a legacy from his mother, whom Jonathan called the most negative woman in the world. Belle Page was a person born at the wrong time in the wrong place, as far as he was concerned. A smart woman who never went to college, she was stuck in a suburban ranch house, bored out of her mind with two children who refused to adhere to her notion of normalcy. First there was Jonathan, with his overly meticulous tastes, his abhorrence of sports, and love of design and fabric. Then there was his sister, Carla, with a body that developed early, and who rebelled as soon as she was able. While Jonathan stayed home and played on the sewing machine, Carla was out every night sleeping with any boy she could seduce. He had once found a steno pad where she'd annotated her conquests, and he stopped reading at 41.

Belle took her daughter's promiscuity personally, as an indictment of her child rearing and a slap in the face of her Catholic morals. There were screaming matches, embarrassing in their intensity and volume. Once, the screaming had brought a police officer to their door.

Their father, Henry, was different—more tolerant, softer and forgiving—but he'd been locked up in his own prison at the real-estate office where he'd worked his life away trying to make enough money to support this unholy cast of characters.

Meanwhile, Jonathan sat at the sewing machine or drew on the back of wallpaper rolls and developed serial crushes on his shop teacher, the mailman, and the clerk at the 7-Eleven. He couldn't wait to leave home, and his mother didn't pretend she was going to miss him. His effeminate side embarrassed her.

"I don't need any more café curtains. Why aren't you playing ball? Go outside and get dirty, for Christ's sake."

She helped arrange early admission to college in his senior year of high school. There was one spectacular fight when she found incriminating magazines under his bed, but that was the only time his sexual preferences were ever mentioned. Still, that had been bad enough. "You're a little freak—I always knew it. I'm humiliated to be your mother!"

"Not as humiliated as I am by you," Jonathan said, slamming the door in her face.

Still, he had never been able to leave his mother completely. Sometimes he even heard her voice issuing from his own mouth. When he put someone down or made a tart or cutting remark, there she was again. Belle . . . why had he thought he could ever be free of her?

After their fight, he vowed to never call her again after their fight, and he hadn't. He considered it once, after he'd gone blind and lost nearly everyone in his life. But then he thought better of it. If he hadn't kept in touch when he was happy, why would he do it when he was sad? And there was no way to get near his father without going through her. There were a few brief phone calls over the years, when an aunt or cousin died, but other than that, they were nearly strangers.

As for his sister, the last he'd heard, she was in Seattle doing something with an organic farm. He found this hard to envision, but it sounded better than her previous activities. Frankly, he had always been bored by her.

So much for family.

In a way, he was glad Lupe had interrupted his reverie.

CHAPTER 5

Later that week, Lupe was in Jonathan's apartment again, this time dusting knickknacks while he sat at his desk signing prints. She found his apartment fascinating, with its rows of books, artifacts, and dozens of paintings, many covered with fabric.

Her progress was slow because she studied each item and couldn't resist asking Jonathan about many of them.

"This egg, is it made out of pure marble?"

"I'm paying you to dust."

"Just tell me."

"Yes. I got it in Greece."

"Greece," Lupe repeated, in a voice that suggested she wasn't sure where this was.

"Yes, Greece, the cradle of civilization. I used to go to Aegina, a small island in the Mediterranean, southwest of Athens. What do you learn in geography? How to get to LA?"

"We don't learn geography," she replied.

"No kidding."

"And this naked lady with no arms?" "That's the *Venus de Milo,* one of the most famous statues in the world."

Lupe silently studied it.

"I like this one with wings that go back."

"That's *Winged Victory,*" Jonathan said as he continued signing. "There's a world art book on my shelf at the end. Why don't you take it home and look at it if you're so interested? But first do the goddamn job I'm paying you for. And no singing!"

"Really? You'd let me do that?"

"What good do books do me now?"

Lupe found the book and held it for a minute, hesitating.

He raised his head, as if trying to discern where she was. "Lupe?"

"Yes?"

"Do you think you can handle these print orders for me? Every two weeks I get a big shipment of them to sign. Some of them are pretty big."

"Yes, I can handle it. I'm strong."

"What's your schedule like?"

"Well, I'm in school."

"Can you drop out? This is more important."

Lupe laughed. "I'll come here right after. I promise."

"What school is it, anyway?"

"Our Lady of Mercy."

"Who teaches you? Nuns?"

"Mm-hmmm."

"I find nuns terrifying."

"Not me. I like them."

"You like them? Well, we'll work on that."

A few minutes later, Lupe finished dusting, and Jonathan handed her some money.

"Go read your book."

◇　◇

The next day, Lupe opened the apartment door to the sound of Jonathan yelling into the phone.

She entered quietly.

Jonathan was wearing a robe and pacing furiously, holding an unlit cigar.

"Settling is out of the question. My work *cannot* be used without my permission. Absolutely not!"

Lupe left the room and began cleaning the bathroom.

"Well, to hell with that. I say no!"

As Lupe scoured the sink, she hummed one of her songs. Suddenly her hand slowed. She walked into the living room as Jonathan continued his rant.

"I don't care if it's a hospital! They charge for their services; I charge for mine!"

Lupe nudged Jonathan. "Do you have any Post-it notes?" she whispered.

Annoyed at her interruption, he covered the receiver. "Over on the desk. Don't interrupt me again. And don't move things around. I can't find a thing!"

Lupe got the Post-it notes from the desk and wrote, *"Only Good Lies Before Me."* She placed it on the wall. Then she began writing others.

Finally, she went back and stuck a note to the middle of Jonathan's bathroom mirror.

She stepped back and looked at herself, smoothing her unruly hair and peering into her own eyes.

Jonathan was off the phone, still muttering to himself.

"Mr. Jonathan?"

"What?"

"I know you're blind, but do you have any idea what I look like?"

He turned toward her for a moment.

"Why do you ask?"

She blushed. "I was just wondering. My grandmother says I'm pretty, but she's the only one. The girls at school, they don't treat me so good. So I was thinking, maybe it's because I'm ugly."

"You're not ugly. I can assure you of that."

"How do you know?"

"I know, that's how. You have an aura around you. And it's not ugly."

"Aura? I think I heard my grandmother say that word once."

"Yeah, I'll bet. Come here. Let me feel your face."

Lupe walked straight up to him and let him move his long fingers over the contours of her face.

"I was also a sculptor, so I know faces very well." He continued moving his fingers, ending up at her forehead. "See, a face should be divided horizontally into three equal spaces. Leonardo da Vinci knew this, and even the ancient Greek mathematicians did. Your face is like that. It has perfect classical proportions. In other words, you're pretty, Lupe. Don't let anyone tell you otherwise."

Lupe looked up at him as if she might cry.

"Thank you. I'll go now."

She walked out of the room, and as she closed the door, Jonathan heard her exclaim, "Classical!"

◇   ◇

Later that week, Lupe stood in the school auditorium at choir practice with a group of popular girls.

As a nun led them in singing "How Great Thou Art," Lupe's soprano voice rang out clear and strong.

This was a cause of general mirth for the popular girls, especially Brie, who rolled her eyes. Lupe stood alone on a separate bleacher row, while the other girls clustered together around Brie, clearly the alpha in the group, responsible for the shunning of Lupe.

After the first song was over, the nun tapped her baton.

"Girls, move together. Why are you divided up like this? All the sopranos in one group. Let's go."

The popular girls looked to Brie, who lowered her eyes as they reluctantly spread out on the bleachers.

Lupe pretended not to notice. She kept a half smile of graciousness on her face and murmured, so no one else could hear, *"I love myself; therefore, I behave and think in a loving way to all people, for I know that that which I give out returns to me multiplied."*

◇   ◇

In Jonathan's apartment that afternoon, Lupe put away the groceries she had brought while Jonathan stood by the window.

"Mr. Jonathan?"

"Yes?"

"There's something I always wondered."

"What?"

"Why are so many of your paintings covered up with sheets so no one can see them?"

Jonathan scowled at the question. "Next time you go to the store, buy some duct tape so I can place it over your mouth when you ask questions like that."

"Okay."

Jonathan sighed. "For one thing, I can't see them anyhow. For another, I don't want to damage them with cigar smoke and sunlight."

"Those don't sound like good reasons." Lupe said. She moved to Jonathan's desk, where there was a particularly large covered canvas. "Plus, you don't even smoke in here."

"Why don't you mind your own business?" Jonathan began, moving toward her. When he realized where she was standing, he stopped short and stood for a long moment. "That one above my desk," he said. "That's my dog, Beau. He was the smartest, most loyal—"

"He *was?* He's gone now?"

"Yes."

"And what about the one next to it, by the window?"

"My parents."

"They gone, too?"

"They're gone, but not dead. They live in Florida—practically the same thing."

"You don't go see them?" Lupe asked.

"No, my mother and I had a fight many years ago. I never liked her much, nor she me. We've barely been in touch for years."

"That's sad," Lupe said. "I wish I could see my parents."

Jonathan hesitated. "I never thought about you having parents. I thought your grandparents took care of you."

"I still have parents. Everybody has parents."

"So why are you with your grandparents?"

Lupe turned. "Maybe you need some duct tape, too."

Jonathan chuckled. "Touché. Do you know what that means?"

Lupe shook her head, and then realized he couldn't see her. "No."

"It means, *You got me.*"

Jonathan turned away and headed toward the kitchen. He turned on the kettle to make a cup of tea.

"So what about the painting in your bedroom?"

Jonathan turned off the gas and stood for a second.

"That one is of my . . . wife."

"Oh—is she gone, too?"

Jonathan nodded.

"In Florida?"

"No, she died. First her, then our baby."

"Your baby?"

"Beau, he was our baby. That's how we felt about him anyhow."

Lupe hesitated. "You mean you and your wife couldn't have any real babies? I knew a lady like that. She took all these injections at the hospital, and then she had these tiny creatures put inside her that they made in a lab, but none of those worked either."

Jonathan had a strange look on his face. He shook his head.

"Did Beau look like you?" Lupe asked. "My dog, Bonita, people said she looked like me."

Jonathan's face brightened. "I don't think so. Nobody ever said so anyhow. He was a boxer, fawn colored, and all muscle. What happened to Bonita?"

"Nothing happened to her. She's in Mexico."

"Mexico?" Jonathan said. "So, that's where you're from?"

"Yes," Lupe said curtly. For the first time, there seemed to be topics she didn't want to talk about.

"And that's where your parents are?"

"Yes, with Bonita. Why don't you get another dog?"she asked.

Jonathan seemed lost in thought.

"I couldn't take care of it," he said quickly. "I can barely take care of myself."

"That's what Grandma says when I ask for another dog."

"What?"

"Who'll take care of it?"

Jonathan looked confused. "Well, *you'd* take care of it, wouldn't you?"

Lupe moved out into the hallway and was suddenly gone.

CHAPTER 6

Riding home from school on her bike the next afternoon, Lupe passed one of the town's most impressive homes, a gabled three-story Victorian, dripping with lacy gingerbread trim and painted pale yellow. Of all the houses in town, this was Lupe's favorite.

When she rode her bike past, she liked to slow down and imagine what it would be like to live there with all the room in the world, a vast emerald yard, and a swimming pool barely visible behind a row of evergreens. Through the large living-room window, she could see a chandelier and two giant portraits, hung next to each other, of a mother and daughter, looking almost like twins. Even the items they threw away were better than what Lupe owned—perfectly good wicker chairs, slightly damaged dolls, and once a checker game still sealed in a box. Her hands itched to peek at these, but she made herself ride on.

Today as she coasted by, she saw the mother and daughter from the portraits pull up the drive in a shiny black car, music blaring from the stereo. It was Brie with her mother, an older replica of the daughter, both of them in sweatpants and ponytails. Lupe stared at them steadily as she coasted by.

Brie's mother said, "Do you know her?"

"God, no," Brie said. "She goes to my school, that's all."

"These Hispanics, sometimes they stake out a house so they can come back later and break in."

Brie sneered, matching her mother's look. "I wouldn't doubt it."

"I hope she isn't stalking you. None of the girls like her, do they?"

"Of course not. She's a joke."

✧ ✧

Lupe arrived at Jonathan's house with groceries, packages, and postage. A routine was being established. Jonathan left the door open now, so Lupe didn't even have to knock.

"I don't know if I can afford you," Jonathan said as he was making out another grocery list to give her.

"But I'm not expensive, and look, I can do everything—clean and shop. I can even cook for you if you want."

"No, thanks. That's all I need—to be charged with violating child-labor laws."

"I'm not a child!"

Jonathan turned his head toward her. "Of course, you're not. Eleven is ancient. Do you have any idea how old I am?"

"Fifty-five."

Surprised, Jonathan asked, "How'd you know that?"

"I looked you up. On Google."

"You did? And what else did you find out?"

"Oh, lots. That you are an important man, a painter. That you had bad luck. That you're blind."

"I *used* to be an important painter."

"That doesn't change," Lupe said. "Plus, you'll paint again."

Jonathan gave a bark of disbelieving laughter. "And how would I manage that? My world is completely dark, in case you haven't noticed."

"You're gonna make new paintings anyhow."

There was a knock on the door, and it swung open to reveal her grandmother. "Lupe, we need you over here with Grandpa."

Lupe headed toward the door.

"Bye, Mr. Jonathan. See you tomorrow."

Jonathan gave her a brief wave, but otherwise he did not stir. He sat staring sightlessly at a pile of prints he was preparing to sign. Lupe's words—"You'll paint again"—had stunned and unnerved him.

❖   ❖

The Saldanas's apartment couldn't have been more different from Jonathan's. It was saturated with a smell that was hard to place, but Lupe thought it might be a combination of mothballed clothes, melted cheese, and the sweet lily of the valley talc her grandmother used after bathing.

On the living-room wall was a single painting, a large print of a pierced and bleeding Jesus. It was ancient and had been brought from Mexico, someone told her once. Lupe's room was essentially a closet, her little bed wedged in a corner, covered with a hand-sewn quilt. When she got out of bed, she entered the hallway; she had no other choice. Her parents' old room, just as small, had been immediately taken over as the household closet and was already jammed with a vacuum cleaner, worn suitcases, and medical equipment.

Lupe assisted her grandmother in changing the bulky oxygen tank that her grandfather carried across his chest. He was sitting in a wheelchair with his eyes closed, looking gray faced and exhausted.

"Here, let me," Lupe said, as her grandmother struggled to hook the breathing tubes back into his nose.

"There, Grandpa. Now you can breathe better. Breathe in deep," Lupe said.

"*Gracias*, sweetheart," he said in a hushed, gravelly voice. He relaxed visibly as he took long breaths through his nose.

Lupe leaned over and kissed him. "I love you— you know that, Grandpa? Lupe loves you."

Tears moved slowly down his leathery face.

"Don't cry. There's no reason to cry."

"You're an angel, Lupe," he said. "As soon as you were born, everyone knew it!"

Lupe smiled. "That's not what I heard. Mama said I cried the whole first year!"

"Still, you are my angel," he said.

From the kitchen, Lupe's grandmother called, "Lupe, why don't you take some dinner over to Mr. Jonathan? I don't think I've ever smelled anything cooking in the house."

"He never cooks! I don't know how he stays alive."

◇   ◇

Lupe carried in an aluminum foil casserole dish into Jonathan's apartment and placed it on the table.

Jonathan sniffed the air. "What's that?"

"Your dinner. We made it over in our kitchen. You're not eating enough, I notice. Mexican food is tasty and full of protein."

"Really? So that's what I've been smelling over on your side of the hall. Tasty proteins. What is it exactly?"

"Carnitas, pork cooked in its own fat, and chicken with mole sauce made of chocolate, chiles, and spices. And a little dish of ceviche: raw fish with spices."

Jonathan made a face. "I was just planning to have some nice crackers with cheese, thanks."

Lupe said nothing, but her disappointed silence was eloquent.

"Maybe I'll try it later," Jonathan said. "I'm not hungry right now."

"You'll just put it in the garbage," Lupe said, as she took off the foil, fixed him a plate, and placed it in front of him.

"Good idea."

"I thought you were a big traveler who's had food from all over the world."

"I used to be." Jonathan took the plate and very delicately picked up a piece of carnitas with his fork, as if it were poison. He took a bite and chewed slowly, and then he took another. "You said this was duck?"

"No. Pork. In its own fat."

"*In its own fat . . .* what are you trying to do, give me a heart attack? That would top off my condition."

"Grandpa eats it all the time. And look at him."

"Right. Exactly my point."

"He's seventy-one!" Lupe said indignantly.

"Is he? Well, that *is* impressive." He licked his fingers. "Not bad."

"Try the ceviche."

"Anything raw makes me nervous."

"This is different—it's really good."

"All right, one bite." He took a tiny shrimp. "I like the spices," he said, chewing. "Although I'll probably be sick for a week."

Without a word, he started on the chicken with mole sauce. "Georgie and I never made it to Mexico. And I've always regretted it." He seemed to be talking to himself.

In five minutes, the plate was clean.

"Thank you. That was good. And interesting."

Lupe beamed with pride.

"Now, next time let me take you to my kind of restaurant—well, what *used* to be my kind of restaurant."

"You don't have to, Mr. Jonathan."

"I know, but I'd like to. I'd get permission from your grandparents, of course. I haven't been there in ages. When can you go? How about Friday?"

"Okay, I'll check with Grandmother. I don't know if she'll let me."

"Why not?"

"Friday's my birthday."

"Yeah? You're what? Ten?"

"I'll be twelve."

"I can't even remember what twelve felt like."

"They were going to have a little party for me, but not until Saturday."

"Well, that's perfect, then. Tell her she can come, too."

"No, she doesn't like fancy places." Lupe gathered her things and moved to the door. "I'll let you know."

❖ ❖

Friday night, Jonathan stood in the court-yard, waiting beside a taxi with William, a local driver. He was bald and squat with an expressive, friendly face.

Finally Lupe came clomping down the stairs.

"What are you wearing? Horse shoes?"

"My mother's good shoes—she left them here. They're too big, but I stuffed them with paper."

"That's sophisticated."

"*Hola*, Lupe," William said. "You look nice tonight."

Jonathan turned to him. "Does she? Describe how she looks, William."

"Well, she's got on a blue dress with white flowers and a blue bow in her hair and white shoes with many straps."

Lupe got in the back of the cab next to Jonathan. "I'm nervous about this fancy restaurant. I've never been to one before."

"Use your positive thoughts!"

"Stop making fun of me!"

"See yourself enjoying it. That's what you tell me, isn't it?"

Lupe looked at him. "I didn't think you ever listened to me."

"Oh, I *listen* to you," Jonathan said. "I don't want to, but I force myself occasionally."

He leaned forward and said, "Fleur de Lys, William. We have a seven-o'clock reservation. But give us the visiting-aunt tour first; we're early."

"You got it."

"William's been driving me around ever since I lost my sight," Jonathan told Lupe.

"That's nice. Sometimes he drives us, too," Lupe said. "I guess you drive everyone, right, William?"

"No, not everyone. Just the cream of the crop, like you two."

"William used to be an actor," Jonathan said in a fake whisper.

"You *did?*"

"A hundred years ago. Before you were born."

"What were you in?"

"TV shows. *Route 66, Hawaii Five-0.* Have you ever heard of them?"

"Yes!" Lupe said. "I've heard of both."

William laughed. "I doubt that, but you're cute when you lie."

He drove them using a circuitous route that ended up taking over an hour.

Jonathan sat back while Lupe oohed and aahed over Chinatown, Fisherman's Wharf, City Hall, and Nob Hill.

"So many hills!" she kept saying.

The last stop was at an ocean beach.

"Can we stay here for a minute?" Lupe asked.

"Sure."

She opened the door and got out.

"What's she doing?" Jonathan asked.

"Just standing there."

"Looking out?"

"Yeah. Looking out at the water."

Lupe eventually got in, bringing the tang of ocean air in with her.

"I never really saw the ocean before," she said simply. "Just on an airplane, looking down."

Her voice sounded as if she might have been crying, but Jonathan was reluctant to ask.

"Okay, William, we're ready now. Let's go eat."

◇   ◇

It was an evening of wonders for Lupe, beginning when the French chef came out and shook Jonathan's hand and then led them through a room draped with sumptuous fabric, walls decorated with modern art, and crystal on the tables. Lupe looked as if she had fallen into a dream.

"Say something," Jonathan said, once they were seated in a private alcove.

"It is so nice, like for the pope or someone holy!" she exclaimed, making Jonathan laugh.

"This is calamari with sweet sauce," the waiter said after Jonathan had ordered from a special menu.

"I never saw this before," Lupe said, examining a piece. "Look, this has suction cups and tentacles like an octopus plus a spider."

A woman beside them with pearls around her thin neck gave them a dirty look.

"It *is* a kind of octopus," Jonathan said softly. "It's squid."

"Oh!" Lupe said on a sinking note and audibly chewed a piece. Jonathan wished, not for the first time, that he could see her face.

"In the salad are pale green soft pieces of something," she said later.

"Give me one."

"Open up," Lupe instructed and then put a forkful in his mouth.

"Artichoke hearts."

"Oh, yes, this I know from home. They're pretty plants. And what is this white meat?"

"Veal."

"From what animal?"

"Never mind. And beside that is broccoli rabe. It's good for you."

But while Lupe seemed enthralled with the scrumptious meal—all four courses of it—Jonathan had the distinct feeling that she wasn't eating it all.

"Lupe, you couldn't have eaten all those garlic rolls. Where are they?"

"I have a little bag. Down here, in my purse. I'll take it home—they'll throw them out if we leave them."

"That's not done in a place like this."

"Well, I'm doing it."

"So, do you like the food? You haven't said."

"Jonathan, this is food for queens. I love it, but . . . it's too good for me."

"No, it's not. That sounds like something I would say."

"It's true!"

"No, I want you to say, *'I'm enjoying the food because I deserve it!'* Say it!"

She smiled. "Okay. I am enjoying this food because I deserve it."

"Thatta girl. Happy birthday, Lupe."

Lupe looked at him and laughed. "Thank you."

CHAPTER 7

The next afternoon, Lupe dusted while Jonathan put away groceries. They moved around each other like an old-time couple, accustomed to being in each other's realm.

"I got the wheat crackers instead of the cheese ones," Lupe said. "They were on sale, plus they are better for you. For the fiber."

"Thanks, Mother."

"Same with spaghetti. Whole wheat, not white."

"When did you become a registered dietitian?"

"I have a nutrition class at school," Lupe said proudly.

"Too bad they don't throw in a little geography, too."

Lupe continued to dust and ended up by Jonathan's desk. "I left you an invitation here."

"For what?"

"You'll see—"

"I *won't* see. How do you expect me to read it?"

"Here," Lupe said. "Just try."

Jonathan took the piece of paper and felt how Lupe had carefully cut out construction paper so that each letter had a texture he could feel.

"You made this for me?"

"Yes, for my choir concert."

Jonathan's face softened for a moment, then hardened again. "Well, number one, I don't like to go out; and number two, I hate choirs."

"Why?"

"Singers always make fish faces when they sing."

"I thought you couldn't see."

"I *remember*, okay? And I don't like the way conductors make those dramatic zipper moves at the end, like this—"

He pinched his forefingers and thumb together and moved his hand horizontally.

Lupe laughed. "Well, you won't be able to see that, either."

"I remember."

"You can just listen to me sing. You'll like it."

"I can hear you sing here whenever I swear. Why should I pay to sit in an auditorium?"

"You haven't sworn in a while, Mr. Jonathan."

"Don't remind me, you little sh—"

Lupe began humming one of her songs.

She got the vacuum from the closet and turned it on.

Jonathan covered his ears. "Go somewhere else with that. It gives me a headache."

She moved into the bedroom. As she vacuumed by the covered canvas by Jonathan's bed, a corner of the cloth got sucked in and the bottom corner peeled from the painting, enough for Lupe to see that the painting of Jonathan's "wife" was of a man.

Lupe stopped, and then a light went on in her head. When she'd first come to San Francisco, her grandmother had explained about men like Jonathan after she and Lupe had sat behind a couple in the subway and watched the younger man lean over and kiss the older one on the neck.

"Love is love," she told Lupe. "This is how it is for some people. We cannot judge. They are hurting no one."

"But, Grandma," Lupe said later, "they are the most handsome ones!"

"It might seem like that," her grandmother said. "But you'll see. There are plenty of handsome men of every kind. You'll find one someday."

Lupe wasn't so sure about that now.

She stared at the painting a moment longer, then walked back into the living room where Jonathan was at his desk, signing prints.

"Mr. Jonathan?"

"What?"

"Don't be mad. But you know that painting of your wife?"

Jonathan stopped signing. "What about it?"

"The vacuum accidentally pulled the sheet off."

Jonathan sat a moment longer and then stood. He headed into the bedroom with Lupe following. He removed the rest of the cover from the painting and sat on the bed.

The painting was of a handsome young man in his 20s, elegantly dressed in a brocade vest, his pale hair combed back from a noble forehead. He held a champagne flute in one hand, gesturing in a way similar to the man in *The Dancing Vagabond.* In the background stood the shadow of an older man, partly turned away and looking out a window. The mood was enigmatic and brooding.

Lupe sat next to Jonathan. "What was his name?"

"George. I called him Georgie. He was my best friend," he said quietly.

Lupe nodded. "His face is nice. I like how he's standing, all fancy."

"Well, he had a flair, let's say."

"Do you have a flair?"

Jonathan smiled. "Yes, I used to have a major flair."

"I think my uncle has a flair, too."

Jonathan. "Really? What does he do?"

"Works at a Williams-Sonoma."

There was a long pause before Lupe asked, "What happened to Georgie?"

"He got very sick. And then he died."

"Oh, that's so sad." She waited for a moment. "What was he like?"

Jonathan rubbed his eyes. "Full of life and fun. Every day was an adventure with him. He'd be so surprised to find out that he's dead."

"Don't you think he knows?"

Jonathan shrugged. "Anyway, when the sickness came, all that fun and adventure were gone. It was a swift and terrible end."

Lupe listened to him with a serious look on her face. "If a house is filled with love and song, there isn't room for sickness. That's what Grandma says; that's why Grandpa always puts on music."

"If I'd known your little secret, I would have hired a mariachi band," Jonathan said archly. "I'm sure it would have made a big difference in the critical care unit. Honestly, I probably would have tried anything."

"Did you cry when he died?"

"Lupe, enough. Are you in training with Barbara Walters or something?"

"Who's Barbara Walters?"

"Yes, I cried. But I don't anymore. I try not to, anyway. I loved him, and he loved me. The last thing he said to me was 'thank you.'"

"And what did you say?"

"I don't remember."

"Maybe you said 'you're welcome'?"

There was a call from next door, "Lupe, Lupe . . ."

Jonathan, clearly upset, turned away as Lupe's grandmother walked to Jonathan's door.

"Lupe," her grandmother said, "time to go to the hospital."

"Already? I hate going there," she said.

Jonathan turned back to her. "Why does your grandfather have to go?"

Lupe turned away. "See you tomorrow."

✧   ✧

When Lupe entered the apartment, her grandparents were standing in the foyer, already prepared to leave. "Put on your jacket, Lupe. I know it's hard. None of us likes to go."

Lupe went into her room and put on a lightweight jacket. Then they all left the apartment in silence and moved outside to the bus stop. Her grandfather was using a walker.

"Why aren't you in your wheelchair?" Lupe asked him, adjusting his collar.

"It's too much trouble, with the bus," he said.

When they reached the hospital, they entered a long line of exhausted-looking patients waiting for their appointment paperwork. The air conditioner was broken, as were the water fountains. Everyone was complaining.

Once they got their paperwork, they sat in another large, penlike area that was even hotter than the first. Lupe and her grandparents sat in straight-back chairs against the wall. There were dozens of families, many speaking Spanish, others talking languages Lupe couldn't place.

One man held his head in his hands; several children moaned in a parent's arms, as if something inside of them were broken.

"When can we get in?" a young girl asked her mother, but her mother shook her head and said wearily, "I don't know, honey. Please sit still."

Lupe turned her gaze to the vending machine and tried to imagine what she'd buy if she had all the money in the world. But even the vending machines weren't tempting here; only off-brand soft drinks and stale-looking nuts and chocolates that had melted in the heat.

Both her grandparents fell asleep, their heads leaning inward, toward Lupe who had also closed her eyes. She was softly chanting: *I love myself; therefore, I live totally in the now, experiencing each moment as good and knowing that my future is bright, joyous, and secure.*

When a nurse called out their name, both grandparents woke with a start. They all stood and filed into the office, where their information was entered into the computer.

Lupe felt as if they were stuck in a process that they'd repeated hundreds of times. What was the sense of computers if every time you had to provide the same material? But her grandparents showed no sign of being angry. Her grandmother got out a small notebook from her purse and reported all the data asked of her in a pleasant voice. Lupe admired her fortitude and level mood; if she ever got sad or scared, she didn't show it.

Poppy was more emotional. She had once seen him grow so angry that he brought his big fist down on the dining-room table, splitting one of the boards. But he never acted this way in public. His hair was even grayer lately, and much of it had fallen out at some point she hadn't noticed.

"Do all three of you need to be in here?" the nurse asked roughly when it was time to enter the doctor's office.

"Yes," said Lupe's grandmother. "All of us."

CHAPTER 8

A crowd of parents and grandparents were taking their seats in the school auditorium. Lupe's grandmother sat in the front row, wearing a hat and a brightly flowered dress. A long procession of girls walked onstage, one a replica of the other—long pale hair with bangs and dark dresses with white collars. Mrs. Saldana clapped loudly when Lupe entered the stage, trailing in at the end. She was smiling, but clearly out of place.

Her long hair had partly escaped from its elastic and was curling around her face, and her dress was cut from the same bright fabric as her grandmother's.

Lupe tried to stand in tight formation with the other singers, but following Brie's lead, they managed to inch away from her, leaving a space that was visible from the audience, as if she were infectious. Brie's face was steely tonight, without the smirk she usually wore. She seemed to be searching the audience for someone.

The conductor, a tall nun in modern habit, bowed to applause and raised her arms. The girls all turned to her and, at her downbeat, commenced singing "The Lord Is Mighty." As the singing continued, Lupe's voice rose, distinctive among the sopranos: sweet, clear, light, and lyrical. At the end of the song, several of the girls looked over at her in disdain, but Lupe was oblivious.

There was a small commotion in the back as the second song began. A man dressed all in black with a slouched hat was helped into a back seat. Apparently, he was blind.

During the next two songs, Jonathan gradually sat up straighter as he heard Lupe's voice above all the others. Her voice had a high bell-like ring to it, and Jonathan listened carefully.

When the singing ended, the conductor performed the "zipper movement," and Lupe smiled. There was a small commotion in the back—the man in black in the back row had now vanished.

◇　◇

As Lupe walked into the apartment the next afternoon, Jonathan was wrapping up a phone call. He sounded exasperated. "Okay, all right! I agree!"

He hung up the phone and put his head in his hands.

"What's wrong?" Lupe asked.

"My mother's going to be in town this week en route to Hawaii. She insists on coming to visit."

"That's good, isn't it?"

"No, it's not good. I haven't seen her for ages. And I haven't seen her for a reason."

"What's the reason?"

"She drives me nuts! That's the reason. She's a little dynamo of negativity."

"What about your father?"

"He never travels with her. He's glad to be left alone. I don't know if I can take it—I really don't. She's truly an awful woman. She's still trying to fix me up with her girlfriends' daughters."

"I'll help you entertain her."

Jonathan laughed. "That'll be good. She's also a bigot, did I mention that? She'll treat you like the maid."

"I don't mind. I am the maid, in a way."

"You're *not* the maid. You're my . . ."

"Friend?" Lupe said. "Is that hard to say?"

"No, it's not hard. Yes, my friend."

"What day is she coming?"

Jonathan put his head in his hands again. "Thursday."

"The bingo club meets at Grandmother's that day. We'll work something out. I'll help you—"

"The bingo club?"

"All the old people in the neighborhood," Lupe said as she walked out.

◇　◇

On Thursday, Jonathan paced back and forth in front of his front window. "Lupe, I hear some-one—come look."

Lupe emerged from the kitchen with a tray of snacks.

"What's that?"

"Cheese nachos, the specialty of Grandma." She looked out the window. "It's a taxi, but it's not your mother."

"How do you know?

"It's a woman, but she's tiny, and she's wearing some kind of fur, and it looks like she's arguing with the driver."

"Oh, God. It's her!"

"I don't see how someone so tall as you could come out of someone so tiny."

"Well, don't ask her. I'm sure it's a gory story."

He turned to Lupe. "I can't believe how anx-ious I feel. This is just my mother!"

"Mothers are very strong influences."

"How do you know so much at eleven?"

She shrugged as the bell rang. "I just turned twelve."

"Buzz her in," Jonathan said in a hopeless voice.

Lupe buzzed her in twice, and they stood lis-tening to the click of high heels as she climbed the stairs. Lupe opened the door, and they stood wait-ing. Jonathan's mother, Belle, stopped at the top, panting dramatically.

"No elevator. What a *surprise*."

As she breathed, she took in Lupe and Jonathan. Lupe could tell by her mottled hands and sunken neck that Belle was near her grandmother's age, but something had been done to her face so that the skin looked pulled and polished.

"Is this my baby? Is this my blind baby?"

She rushed to Jonathan and wrapped her arms around him, knocking him back into the apartment. She burst into tears. "How could this be? How could you lose your sight so young?"

Jonathan's face was contorted with feeling. He patted her shoulder and dislodged her from his neck. "It was all a long time ago, Mother. I'm used to it by now."

"Well, I'm not! I haven't been allowed to see you—" Her tears suddenly turned off as if with a spigot as she eyed Lupe. "Is this your maid?"

"I told you," Jonathan said to Lupe. "No, this is my friend Lupe. She's been a real help to me."

"A child? I hope you're not having an inappropriate relationship with her."

"No, Mother. Of course not. Unless dusting my apartment is inappropriate to you. Come in and sit down."

Belle sashayed in, looking around the apartment with clear distaste. "This is so small!"

"It's sufficient for me. Can I get you anything? Lupe brought some wonderful hors d'oeuvres."

Belle sat down gingerly on the sofa. "I'll have some plain water, if you can spare it. I'm watching my weight."

Jonathan sat across from her. "Well, how've you been? How's Father?"

Belle sniffed. "If you were really curious, you could have contacted us."

"I had some issues I was handling."

"Yes, I can imagine. And how's your friend—that Georgie person?"

"He died years ago. I told you that. All my good friends died around the same time."

Belle shuddered. "From that ghastly virus. But I always said, if you live a degenerate—"

Lupe interrupted. "Mr. Jonathan has many new friends here in the building. They're getting together today right across the hall." She opened the door, rushed across, and swung open her grandparents' door. The apartment was full of every old-timer in the neighborhood—all sitting on folding chairs, all playing bingo.

"*¡Hola!*" several called out.

Belle rolled her eyes. "*Those* are your friends? They're ancient! And speaking Spanish! So now you hang out with children and elderly illegal aliens?"

Jonathan was staring at the floor; a vein in his forehead had appeared that Lupe had never seen before.

Despite her protestations, Belle took a bite of the nachos and soon had polished off half the dish, while gossiping nonstop. "And Sara Evans—you know she was the last one of us besides me who wasn't divorced—well, as soon as her decree went through, she found out she had brain cancer! And not the curable kind either. I said—"

"I remember Sara, vaguely. She had that terrible plastic surgery on her ears."

"That's the one. You should see her now— her eyelids look melted, like candle wax. She had this new therapy where they heat your skin and supposedly tighten it. But I say, give me an old-fashioned face-lift any day, rather than these new-fangled procedures. They never do what they say they will. And the cost—"

"How's Father's heart?"

Thrown off track, Belle shook her head and looked grim. "Not good. He doesn't eat right. He can't control his own fat intake. The man is eighty-five years old and completely set in his ways, so I can't tell him what to do. Just like you kids. Speaking of which, I *never* hear from your sister. When I think of the money we spent on her education, I find the ingratitude stunning. Not that I expect to be paid back, but I do expect a certain level of respect. And *your* education—why, we'd be millionaires if we'd—"

"I believe my art-school tuition paid off," Jonathan said archly.

"That's a matter of opinion," Belle sniffed.

Lupe, picking up around them, said, "Mr. Jonathan's art is very famous."

"Well, no one *I* know ever hears of him anymore." Belle looked at Lupe suspiciously. "Are you sure there isn't something inappropriate going on with you two?"

"Mr. Jonathan, what does *inappropriate* mean?" Lupe asked.

"In this case, it means a demented mind."

Belle laughed. "That's rich, coming from you."

"Mother," Jonathan interrupted, "how long do you think it's been since I've seen you?"

Belle rubbed her temple. "Oh, I don't know. Many years . . ."

"Well, apparently it hasn't been long enough," Jonathan said.

His mother stared at him with her usual unsympathetic eyes.

"I let you come visit, against my better instincts. But I've been right to avoid you. You're full of negativity, and I just can't afford to be around your energy anymore—"

"My *energy?* Well, I'm sorry. I'm simply being myself."

"I know it's who you are. But who you are and who I am are not compatible. So let's leave it at that. I have to ask you to leave."

"*Leave?* Are you serious? My plane doesn't go for hours. What am I supposed to do?"

"Yes, I'm serious. There's a mall nearby. I'm sure you can find something . . ."

Belle opened her mouth and then shut it again. She picked up her purse, stood, and looked around the apartment one more time. "Your father warned me this wasn't a good idea. I should have listened. But I won't tell him how far you've fallen. He wouldn't believe it."

"Tell him whatever you wish, Mother. He's the one I would've liked to see. I'll call you a cab."

"Don't bother."

"Lupe, would you help my mother out?"

"I don't need help from either one of you," she said, looking narrowly at Lupe.

She walked out and slammed the door.

"*¡Hola!*" another bingo player called out as she huffed by.

"*Hola,* yourself," she said, clomping down the stairs. "I've never been so mortified in my life."

Jonathan stood by the window until the sound of her was gone.

"Mr. Jonathan, are you okay?"

"I didn't think it was possible that she'd be worse than I remembered, but she is. I was hoping I had exaggerated her in my mind."

"She has her good points, I think," Lupe said weakly.

"Name one."

Lupe was silent for too long. "Her purse was nice; also her shoes."

Jonathan laughed. "I think you probably should leave me alone for a while."

Lupe left the apartment and shut the door behind her.

CHAPTER 9

The next day Jonathan returned to the apartment from his monthly doctor's visit to hear salsa music blaring from the upstairs window. He climbed the stairs scowling and then stopped on the landing. The music wasn't coming from the Saldanas's apartment, as he'd supposed, but from his. The door wasn't even closed the entire way. He walked in and heard what sounded like feet scuffling.

"Lupe! What's going on in here?"

The music was lowered. "Sorry, I didn't think you would be home so soon. I was using the music to help get rid of any bad energies. Remember I told you what Grandpa said—about music and love?"

"And what did your grandpa tell you about police complaints?"

"It wasn't that loud. How was your doctor's appointment?"

"The same. I'm always the same."

"No, you're getting better. I can feel it."

"You don't get better from what I have."

"I don't believe that."

She turned up the music again, not as loud as before.

"Lupe—"

"You don't get enough exercise, for one thing," she said. "Come on, let's dance. I was just practicing. Follow me." She grabbed his hand and began pulling him across the room. "I'll lead. You be the follower."

"Lupe, I can't see. I can't dance with you."

"Okay, so just hold my hand so you can feel what I'm doing."

"I feel what you're doing—you're driving me crazy."

She kept hold of Jonathan's hand as she moved around him.

"I feel like a maypole," he said.

"What?"

"Never mind."

The song seemed to go on forever, and when it finally ended, Jonathan let go. "I'm exhausted just being around you."

"There's one more," she said, and sure enough, the music changed. "Cha-cha!"

Lupe took his hand again and began dancing strenuously around him.

Jonathan said, "Georgie used to love the cha-cha. He always tried to get me to do it with him."

"So you didn't dance even when you could see?"

"No, it's just not my thing. It's so . . . I don't know . . . public."

"So, what's wrong with that?" Lupe was panting now. "It's a very good workout for your body. For your spirit, too."

The apartment door had swung open, and Lupe's grandmother and several neighbors were standing out in the hall, watching.

When the song ended, there was a round of applause from the hallway, startling them both.

Jonathan said, "I didn't know there was an audience. We'll have to charge next time."

Lupe laughed and fanned the air with her hand. "It's hot in here. I better go now."

◇ ◇

The doorbell rang later in the week, and Jonathan pushed the buzzer, expecting a delivery.

But when he opened the door, he stopped short and stood silently for a long moment.

"Carla? What is this, old home week?"

"I thought you were blind. How'd you know it was me?"

"It's a family scent. Mother was just here earlier in the week, so it's still fresh in my nose—or mind, or whatever."

"I heard. She called me immediately, in hysterics of course."

"Who's there with you?"

"How'd you know—?" Carla smiled. "Your nephew, my son. Rodney, this is my brother."

"I didn't know you had a son."

"Two, actually. The other, Teddy, is in college."

Rodney stepped forward, slender and pale faced, and gave Jonathan his hand. Jonathan stood holding it for several minutes, and a slow smile grew on his face.

"I'm glad to meet you, really. You're one of the few living creatures who possesses some of my DNA."

"Don't scare him, Jonathan," Carla said. "Can we come in?"

"Of course."

They moved inside and sat down in the living room.

"So," Carla said.

"Yes, so. Why are you here?"

"Blunt as usual. Well, hearing Mother talk about you, I couldn't get you out of my mind. I always think of you as so successful and busy. But from what she said, you're alone so much, with your . . . condition—"

"You mean my blindness."

"Yes."

"Well, that's true, I am alone a lot. And I'm actually glad you came, Carla. Tell me what you've been doing with yourself all this time."

"Oh, not that much. I got married. I had the boys. I got divorced." She laughed. "An old story."

"Rodney, how old are you?"

"Nineteen."

"Truth is, I thought it might be good for Rod to meet you. Actually, he reminds me a lot of you. He likes design and fashion and all that. And he definitely doesn't get that from me."

"How about his father?"

Carla laughed again and waved her hand. When she realized he couldn't see her, she said, "Hardly. He was a sports fanatic. And all my work life has been in banks and bookkeeping, so anything creative is definitely not coming from me."

The boy blushed and looked down at his shoes.

"Well, Rodney, I have all kinds of design and fashion books, and you're welcome to come over and borrow them whenever you want."

Rodney made a small sound of assent. He seemed perpetually embarrassed.

"Why don't you look around? There's probably stuff you'd find interesting."

Rodney got up and wandered into the foyer lined with books; Carla cleared her throat.

"The truth is, Jonathan, Mother and I still don't get along either. She thought my divorce was scandalous, and the boys can't stand being around her. I'm 51 years old, and besides Daddy, you're the only close relative I have."

"You know who your voice sounds like? Aunt Margaret," Jonathan said.

"Oh, God, really?"

"Yes, isn't that weird? You know, the most memorable visual image I have of you is from some fair we went to when we were little, and Mother dressed you in a dotted-swiss sailor suit and patent-leather shoes. It must have been around Easter."

Carla laughed. "I remember that, too. Another of her stupid coordinated outfits. That was always her main concern, whether our outfits matched."

"Do you mind if I feel your face?" Jonathan asked. "I'm curious."

"No, go ahead."

Jonathan got up and ran his fingers over his sister's face.

"I'm old now," she said.

"Yeah, well, so am I."

"Actually, you look better than I was expecting."

"Thanks—I guess," Jonathan said.

"So, as I was saying, I'd like it if we could establish some kind of relationship, if you're interested. I don't mean anything heavy—just be in touch, you know? I only live about 20 minutes away."

"I thought you were in Seattle."

She laughed. "That was years ago."

Jonathan sighed. "You know, I'd like it, too. I'm never going to be able to get along with Mother, although I would like to see Dad."

"Maybe I can arrange something."

"That would be great." Suddenly Jonathan's eyes filled with tears. "I—"

Carla was at his side. "Oh, I didn't mean to upset you."

"It's okay."

Rodney was in the doorway. "What's wrong?"

Carla stood. "Uncle Jonathan just got emotional." She wiped her own eyes. "I guess we'd better go. Can I have your number?"

"Sure—just take it off the phone."

Carla copied the number, then hugged Jonathan. "I'll be in touch. I'm glad I came."

"Me, too. I'm glad to meet you, Rodney. Come again whenever you want."

Lupe was walking in as they left.

"Who is that, Mr. Jonathan?"

"My sister and her gay son."

"Really?"

"Yes. I don't even know if she realizes it. But he does. Will wonders never cease?"

"Does that mean you're glad about it?"

"Yes, I'm glad. I'm not sure why, but I am."

◇　◇

Jonathan was setting the table with an antique bone china tea set when Lupe walked through the door with a bag of groceries.

"I got everything you wanted—tea, cookies . . ."

"What kind?"

"Milano."

"Excellent. How about lemons?"

"Yes, those, too."

"Well, get those out, and I'll show you how I like them sliced."

In fifteen minutes, they were sitting together in the dining room, having formal tea. The table was covered with a linen tablecloth that Lupe had ironed just so, following Jonathan's instructions. The matching napkins were folded and starched. The tea set was edged with gold and embossed with blue pansies. There was a vase of fresh hydrangeas and peonies in the center of the table. Lupe kept walking in and out of the room, admiring the look of everything.

"This looks so pretty, I feel like we shouldn't use it. I wish you could see!"

"I can see it in my mind, as you would say. I had tea like this many times before I was blind."

Jonathan poured with great care, with Lupe strategically moving the items he needed closer.

"So, how many sugars do you take?"

"Umm . . . two? I've never had tea like this before—just iced tea."

"I find that impossible to believe. Anyhow, Georgie took two—occasionally three."

"Because he was sweet. How many do you take?"

"None. Just lemon."

"Ha! That's why you're so sour."

Jonathan gave her a mean face, then poured her some tea.

"So let's hear more about this *quinceañera* dress you keep talking about."

Lupe's face lit up as she began talking in a rush. "I know just what I want. I even dream about it. First of all, I don't like strapless dresses, so I want little thin satin straps and embroidery on the *corpino*."

"What's a *corpino?*"

Annoyed at being interrupted, Lupe said, "The bodice. You don't know anything, do you? Then on the pick-up skirt, lace and beading. I'm still not sure yet about the color or the fabric. But it should be pale, because I think it should look like a wedding dress."

"I have a friend who owns a fabric store. I used to buy everything from him when I had a tailor. He gets fabric from all over the world—the best. We could go over and look sometime."

"Could we? When?"

"Whenever you want—"

"How about tomorrow?"

"Sure, but won't styles change in three years?"

"*Quinceañera* styles never change. Always very elegant. Some girls even wear a tiara."

Jonathan snorted, and tea came out of his nose. "A tiara? Now, that's tacky."

Lupe smiled conspiratorially. "I know. I'm not sure about the veil either. Do you think I should wear one or not?"

Jonathan said, "I don't think so. Veils are to hide behind. But you're pretty. I told you."

"You're the only one who thinks so. The girls at school—especially this one named Brie—they treat me like I'm ugly."

"Brie? She's named after a cheese? What the hell does she know anyway? She sounds like a little snot. Describe her to me."

"Well, she's perfect looking, I mean for our school. Long blonde hair with different shades of streaks in it, pulled back in a low ponytail. And this little nose, that's pushed up—what do you call that?"

"Pig?"

"No pug, I think. And her skin is perfect and tanned even when there's no sun, and she and her mom dress just alike, in short skirts and tight tops that show their stomachs. Plus, they're rich."

"I hate both of them already. They sound dreadful."

"Underneath, I think Brie might be all right. Anyhow, I know I'm going to be her friend."

"And why's that?"

"Because every day I close my eyes and make a little picture in my head of us as friends."

"And you think that's going to work?"

"I know it will."

"I don't understand why you'd even bother with someone like this Brie person. I bet you're prettier than she is anyway. You're going to be what they used to call 'the belle of the ball.'"

"Does that mean pretty?"

"It means pretty and . . . gracious."

Lupe smiled. "I like having tea."

"You know who used to love it when my friend and I had tea? Beau."

"Your dog?"

Jonathan nodded.

"Did you still have him after your friend died?"

"He died three months later. I figured he might; he was so close to Georgie. One day he stopped eating, and then the next day, he wouldn't get out of bed. Soon after that, he left me, just like my friend. It was just about the worst day I ever had. Then it was my turn."

"Your turn?"

"My friend, my dog, my sight, my career." He snapped his fingers. "Gone in a heartbeat. But I still have this lovely tea set, which I haven't used in years. And I still make money off my prints, thank God."

"Do you still paint pictures in your head?" Lupe asked.

"What do you mean?"

"Do you still imagine painting them?"

"No. I don't see anything in my head."

"Maybe that's the problem. If you would—"

Jonathan interrupted, his expression dark. "Oh, I see. It's my fault. I'm awful. I'm doing something wrong. That's why I'm blind, too, I suppose."

"Don't say things like that. There's something in the air that hears what we say."

"Where do you get these harebrained ideas?"

Lupe ignored him and leaned forward. "They're little molecules. When we say something, it gets repeated to all the other molecules in the world. And they work together to make what we say happen to us."

"Well, thank them for making me blind."

"If you paint it or say it, then it happens," Lupe continued, undaunted. "That's why you shouldn't swear or say negative words. And pictures in our head are even stronger. We paint the future with them."

Jonathan was silent for a long moment. "That is the most ridiculous thing I've ever heard."

"Well, I believe it," Lupe said, standing. "Plus, you're not an awful person. An awful person wouldn't have come to my concert."

Before he could respond, she walked out the door.

CHAPTER 10

The next afternoon, Jonathan was waiting for her at the doorway.

"Okay, we're going to look at fabric today. I called my friend."

"I thought you were mad at me."

"I can't stay mad at you for long, unfortunately. C'mon. I already called the cab."

William was waiting at the curb, his engine running.

"Hi, William," Jonathan said as they got in. "We want to go to Wide World of Fabric. Do you know where that is?"

"Sure do. *Hola*, Lupe. How's your grandpa?"

"Okay for an old man—that's what he always says."

"Good, good."

William stepped on the gas, throwing them back into the seat.

They arrived at a storefront with a display window crowded with wedding gowns and prom dresses. Lupe was immediately transfixed.

"Ooh, look at that pink one. I love it," she said as they got out.

"I was going to have you wait, William, but we may be here all week," Jonathan said. "I'll call you for a pick up."

William saluted.

"There he is!" A portly middle-aged man with a measuring tape around his neck emerged from the back. "How are you, Johnny? It's so great to see you."

"Leo." Jonathan bent down and kissed the little man European style, on both cheeks. "This is my friend Lupe, who I was telling you about. She wants to look at fabric for a special dress."

"*¡Muy buena!* Hello there, my dear," Leo said, taking her hand. "I've pulled a selection to show you."

He led them into a room where there were dozens of fabric samples arrayed in a rainbow of colors.

"What's this dress for?"

"My *quinceañera.*"

"A very big day. Well, we have everything, including patterns and fabric galore."

"I've never seen so much material! So beautiful. And look at the pearls and sequins!"

Lupe's eyes glowed as she walked in a circle, touching each fabric as if it were gold.

As she fingered each one, Leo chanted the type of fabric: "Lamé, chiffon, satin, silk, tulle, organza, taffeta, lace."

To Lupe, the names were like a song.

"Oh, I love them all, but this one's the best." She stopped before the palest blue chiffon. Then she examined beads and embroidery webbed in a silvery thread. "Some girls wear bright colors, but I want it to be very pale, like a wedding gown."

"You'll have a wedding someday, too," Jonathan said.

"I don't know," Lupe said.

"Well, why wouldn't you?"

"You didn't have one."

"Well, I'm different."

"Maybe I'm different, too."

Jonathan laughed.

"Let's stick with this at the moment. Let Leo drape it around you, and you can see how the shade is with your coloring."

Lupe went into a fitting room with Leo and came back out with a length of fabric wrapped around her. Lupe stationed herself in front of Jonathan and waited.

"I'm here," she said.

"I know." He was quiet a moment. "There are times when I really wish I could see."

"Me, too."

"Look at yourself and describe it."

Lupe stood looking at herself in the three-way mirror. She turned in all directions. "I need you to help me."

"No, you don't. You can tell me for yourself. Ask Leo if you're not sure."

Leo said, "She looks very beautiful in this color. We call it cloud blue; it has a little shimmer that really complements her skin. I recommend it."

"There you go. Do you want to buy it now?"

"I think I do. I have to see if I've saved up enough money."

"Remember, you don't need it for a while," Jonathan said.

"I know, but I have to plan it. It's my most important future event. I have to see it in my mind."

"Leo, let her see some patterns, then figure out how much it's going to set us back."

Leo said, "Let me measure you, Lupe. And we can pick the style you want, and add some for your growth."

Jonathan sat in a straight-back chair and waited for them to come out of the dressing room.

✧　✧

Lupe's voice was crestfallen. "I'm $380 short," she explained when they returned. "I thought I had enough, but it takes a lot of material. I guess I'll have to wait."

"No, you won't. I'll pay for it, Leo."

"Mr. Jonathan, you can't—"

"Who says?"

"My grandmother will—"

"I'll explain to your grandmother."

"No, I—"

"Lupe, we're buying this. Leo, wrap up everything and send it to my apartment."

"Thank you," Lupe said gravely. "But I'll pay you back. I swear to you, I will. And I'll work double time from now on."

"Please don't," Jonathan said. "You'll drive me nuts."

✧　✧

Jonathan was listening to the news later that evening when his phone rang.

"Yes?"

A long pause, and then: "Johnny? Son?"

Jonathan sank into the chair beside the phone. He felt as if the bones had been removed from his body.

"Are you still there?" the voice asked.

"Dad," he finally said. "After all this time. I can't believe how much family stuff is happening this week."

"Well, that's probably my fault. Your mother told me your number was unlisted and that you'd requested that none of us call you."

"What? That's not true."

"I should have investigated. I didn't need to take her word."

Jonathan sighed, and then fell silent again. He felt as if his mouth couldn't produce the right words. "How are you? Mother said your heart wasn't great."

"Well, I'm eighty-five. That's why I'm calling. I wanted to hear about you while there's still time."

"There was a time when I'd have had a lot to report, but not anymore," Jonathan said. "As you know, I'm blind—and I'm pretty much alone here. I can't paint or do much else. It's not very pretty."

His father said, "I know what you mean. I can't do much either. I get angina whenever I exert myself. Plus, Belle keeps me on a short tether." He sniffed again. "I hear you're living right near the Mission District."

"Yes, I'm in it, really. Most of my neighbors are Hispanic. It's been fine, really."

"I haven't been over there in years. Your mother's scared of it, though I know she came to see you." He stopped and cleared his throat.

"Is there something special you called to say, Dad?"

"I guess I called to say that I'm sorry I wasn't a better father. You were so different, and your mother just couldn't handle it, so I let her set the tone, like I've let her take the lead in everything. I've spent so many years letting her tell me how to feel, and now my life's almost over. I should have been more help to you, especially when you lost your sight. But one thing I can do is look after you in my will. I want you to know that when I'm gone, you'll get a handsome settlement—"

"Dad, I don't want anything—"

"No, this is what I want."

"Really. I should have given *you* money. I'm the one who made money."

"Jonathan, no argument. Your mother doesn't know, and she doesn't need to know. I worked for 40 years at a job I hated; now I'm going to do what I want."

They fell silent again.

"Do you want to get together sometime?" Jonathan managed.

"I don't think I better," his father answered softly. "It would be too hard on me—my heart, like I was telling you."

"Yes. I don't know how strong mine is either."

They both breathed in and out.

"Thanks, Dad. Really."

Suddenly the phone went dead.

Jonathan held the receiver for a few moments longer and then hung up.

◇   ◇

Later that week, as Lupe rode her bike to the grocery store, she stopped suddenly and did a double take. Brie's Victorian house had a for sale sign on the front lawn. Lupe stood there for so long that the lace curtains opened. Brie's mother peeked out, and then pulled them shut again tightly.

Back on her bike, Lupe found herself caught in the middle of a funeral procession. No matter how hard she tried, she couldn't get out of it; she was stuck behind the hearse with a casket visible through the tinted windows, followed by a carload of elderly women, openly weeping.

Since the procession stretched as far she could see, she got off her bike and walked in the procession, head bowed. When the line of traffic turned right toward the cemetery, she got on her bike again and rode straight ahead.

The next day, Jonathan was lying on the couch listening to the news as Lupe put away groceries.

"Mr. Jonathan, do you ever go to the cemetery where your friend is buried?"

"How do you know my friend is buried? He could have been cremated."

"I don't know, just guessing."

"Well, the answer is no."

"No what?"

"I've never been to the cemetery. I can't see, in case you haven't noticed. It was too painful to go right after he died, and now it's too late."

"How about if I take you?"

"Are you going to ride me there on your bike?"

"No, on the bus. I know the public transportation. I could go with you."

Jonathan was silent for a long time. "Did you get more Milano cookies today?"

"Yes, on sale. Two for one."

"Good." He was silent again. "I'll think about it, okay?"

CHAPTER 11

Lupe was in the girl's bathroom stall when she overheard snatches of conversation from two popular girls who were washing their hands.

"I heard Brie's dad got fired for doing something illegal at work. I don't know what. But my mom said it was pretty bad."

"That's why they're selling the house?"

"Yeah, plus I heard they have to move into an *apartment*. Can you imagine? I'd be so embarrassed . . ."

When Lupe emerged from the stall, the two girls clammed up and dried their hands, avoiding her eye. Suddenly, Brie entered the room.

"Hey," she said, somewhat tentatively, as the two girls brushed by her in silence, "are you two going to Cooper's?"

The girls ignored her question as they left.

Brie's face fell, and she stepped into a stall and locked the door.

Lupe stood a moment studying Brie's feet under the stall; then she washed her hands and left.

✧　✧

Lupe disembarked from a metropolitan bus and waited at the bottom as a long arm extended. She reached up and took Jonathan's hand as he got off the bus behind her.

Jonathan used a cane and held on to her arm as they walked. He was dressed in a pale linen suit and an elegant hat. Lupe was wearing the tropical dress she had worn at her choir concert. They walked down a street, which grew progressively less crowded and became semiresidential. On the right stood a sign—WOODLAWN CEMETERY.

They walked together under a stone arch, and Lupe looked at a badly photographed map. "Section P, row five."

Jonathan didn't speak, but kept holding her arm. They walked silently through row after row of monuments.

Lupe swallowed. She had never been in such a huge cemetery before. She found it unsettling that each of these monuments represented a human life that had come and gone.

"There's so many—as far as the eye can see," she said.

"Tell me about some of them."

"There are a lot of tablets . . . you know, just monuments with the names drilled in," Lupe said.

"Read me one."

"Okay. 'Beloved brother and husband, Marvin Rednick, 1925–1995. Rest in Peace.'"

"Original," Jonathan said.

"'We love you, Mother, Sally Dunn, 1909–1999.' That's a long life."

"Too long, if you ask me."

"Here's section P."

They turned.

"These are more fancy. There's more angels and all."

"I'm not surprised."

As they walked along, there was an odd lack of human sound, only lawnmowers and birdsong, and the sweet scent of flower bouquets strewn over the most recent graves, the ones Lupe avoided.

Soon they were surrounded by monuments of angels and weeping women. Lupe stopped stockstill. She had located Georgie's grave; next to it was another monument with the date left blank:

Jonathan Page, 1956–

"Here it is," she said quietly.

"Where?"

"Right in front of us."

He walked forward and touched the headstone, a weeping woman, her hair thrown over her face, bent in lament. His fingers examined the stone.

"This feels like what I wanted."

"You picked it out?"

"I had it commissioned. I saw it in progress, but not when it was finished." He paused. "Would you read some other names?"

Lupe looked at the surrounding area. "Okay. Arthur Hill, Lee Jones, Bradley Foster, Larry Jones, Peter Simon . . ."

Jonathan bowed his head. "My friends. They're all here together. I didn't realize."

Lupe was silent.

Jonathan said, "Would you mind leaving me alone for a while? Just take a walk and come back."

"Will you be okay?"

"Of course I'll be okay. I can just sit down somewhere here."

"Here's a bench." She steered him toward a stone bench nearby, and he situated himself facing Georgie's monument.

Lupe walked slowly and reluctantly around the cemetery. She sat for a while under a tree, closed her eyes, and began murmuring in Spanish. A groundskeeper drove by and looked at her suspiciously.

He stopped his riding mower. "Are you okay?"

Lupe opened her eyes. "Yes."

He moved on, and she closed her eyes again.

When she opened them again, she looked at her watch and returned to the section where she'd left Jonathan.

He'd taken off his sunglasses and hat and was leaning to one side. It wasn't until she moved closer that she realized that he had been talking, conversationally, to the monument.

"Mr. Jonathan."

He looked up, red-faced. It was the first time she'd seen his eyes this closely. They were milky white, fixed, and filled with liquid. "I told you to leave me alone."

"The next bus comes in twenty minutes, and then there isn't another one for an hour."

"Okay," he said brusquely. "Help me up." He still seemed annoyed.

"I didn't mean to interrupt."

"You always interrupt, Lupe. That's what you're best at. That's all you've done since I met you."

✧ ✧

In physical education class, a group of miserable-looking girls, including Lupe, stood outside the school in their ill-fitting gym costumes.

The phys ed teacher, a blocky middle-aged woman, was dividing up the girls into teams.

"Okay, girls, I know soccer isn't easy, but let's try a game."

The girls moaned.

"Alisa, you head up one team; Lupe, you've got the other. Pick your members—eleven each. Alisa, pick the first five."

Alisa, one of the most popular girls, called out several of her crowd. "Heather, Ashley, Laura, Jeanie, Tanya."

She pointedly ignored Brie, who stood apart, looking extremely uncomfortable.

When it was Lupe's turn, she looked around a moment, and then said, "Brie, Lily, Sandra, Lisa, Karen."

Brie looked relieved but slightly embarrassed as she walked over to Lupe's side.

Once the game began, Lupe came alive on the field. She was the only girl on her team who seemed to remember the rules. The rest of them were bumbling and confused. She scored one goal, then another, assisting Brie whenever she faltered.

The girls on the other team were even worse— out of shape and disoriented. One of them tripped and fell; one collided with another player. Lupe continued to propel the ball toward her opponents' goal, passing to Brie.

"Come on, Lupe—one more and we've got it!" one of the girls whispered.

Lupe scored, and the team exploded with cheers.

The teacher blew her whistle. "Okay, great job, Lupe! You play like a pro."

Lupe's team clustered around her.

Brie asked admiringly, "How'd you get to be so good at soccer?"

By now Lupe was breathless and leaning over; it was clear that she had overdone it in her zeal. "We used to play in Mexico all the time."

✧ ✧

When Lupe entered the library the next afternoon, all the computers were taken again. Brie was sitting at one of them.

This time, when she saw Lupe, she began gathering her papers.

"I'm done—you can have this," she said.

"Oh, that's all right—" Lupe began.

"No, I mean it. I'm finished."

Lupe could see that Brie had been on a social networking site, peppered with photographs and dialogue.

"Do you want me to leave it on Facebook?" Brie asked her.

"No, I'm not on that," Lupe said. "I don't know enough people."

Brie considered this as she stood holding her books in front of her.

"You should try it. If people see you're on, they might friend you."

Lupe tried to hide her shock at Brie's cordial tone. "Okay. Maybe I'll try it."

Brie walked out, and Lupe sat down and began doing her homework.

When she got home that night, Lupe walked directly into the kitchen where her grandmother was cooking rice.

"Grandma, I know I asked you once before, but do we have enough money to buy a laptop computer now?"

Mrs. Saldana turned to her with a serious face. "Lupe, you know we don't. We barely have the money to buy food."

"I keep imagining we have more money, but it's not working."

"Well, keep at it," her grandmother said, stirring. "Nothing happens overnight. Ask Mr. Jonathan if you can use his computer."

❖ ❖

Lupe rapped on his apartment door and let herself in.

"Hey, Mr. Jonathan, can I use your computer for a minute?"

"Go ahead."

She sat down at his desk, in front of his big monitor.

"It's got the audio component turned on, so I'll be able to hear what you're doing."

"I don't care. It's nothing dirty or anything."

She typed for a while, and the words *This is Facebook* were intoned. Next, silence.

"You're getting on that stupid site? I don't believe it."

"Just for a minute."

She sat there in silence. Then there were more words: *Brie Heartland requests that you be her friend.*

After a beat:

Becca Zolinsky requests that you be her friend.
Lee Hanley requests that you be her friend.
Danny Miller requests that you be his friend.

"Wow," Lupe whispered, as she pushed *agree* for each one. They all were students in her class.

"Did I hear the name Brie Heartland in conjunction with the term *friend*?" Jonathan asked.

"Yes," Lupe said. "You did."

CHAPTER 12

The next day, Jonathan lay on the couch listening to the radio, a pensive look on his face, while Lupe rattled around in the kitchen.

"Mr. Jonathan, I forgot to tell you, I can't come tomorrow. I have a test."

He lowered the radio. "That's okay. I don't need you all the time."

He reached back again to turn up the radio, and a piece of paper fluttered down onto his face. "What's this?" He touched the wall and felt another one. "And this?" He felt them gingerly. The wall was covered with what felt like Post-it notes. "Why are there pieces of paper all over my wall?"

Lupe came to the doorway. "It's just an extra thing I do."

"What's that supposed to mean?"

"Well, I know you don't have good pictures in your head or say positive things about yourself, so I do it for you. I put them there because that's where you sit."

Jonathan sat up and felt up and down the wall.

"There's more on the bathroom mirror."

"Oh, for God's sake." Jonathan stomped into the bathroom, clearly annoyed. "What do these stupid things say?"

"Different things. *Only good lies before me. I'm going to get my sight back.* Or *I create my own future.* Things like that. But most of them say *I'm going to paint a lot more beautiful pictures.*"

"Lupe, I'm not getting my sight back, no matter what kind of mumbo jumbo you hang on my walls."

"Don't say that. The molecules will hear you."

Jonathan grew increasingly angry. "I don't *believe* in your molecules, okay? And I'm getting tired of hearing about them all the time. Bad things happen. They happened to *me.* And all the wishful thinking in the world can't do anything about it."

"You don't have to believe in the sun for it to still shine on you."

Jonathan erupted. "And you don't have to believe in disease for it to come along and devastate your life and take away everyone you love. Ask your grandfather. Have the molecules and the Post-it notes worked for him? Have they stopped whatever is eating him alive?"

Lupe's faced collapsed. There was a long silence.

"I'm sorry. That was an awful thing to say."

More silence.

"I said I'm sorry—really."

More silence.

Jonathan put a hand out in front of him. Lupe wasn't there. The door was left open. He turned around and ran into an umbrella stand. He kicked it out of the way.

✧   ✧

The next day, Jonathan heard a commotion outside in the hall and opened the door. Lupe's grandmother emerged, rushed and harried. As she left, she called back into the apartment.

"I call you as soon as I can, sweetheart." She ignored Jonathan and hurried down the stairs, weeping audibly.

She collided with Mrs. Ramirez, the downstairs neighbor, and the two of them spoke in frantic Spanish for a moment.

"Shit—it must be Mr. Saldana," Jonathan whispered to himself. He went across the hall and knocked. "Lupe, it's me . . ."

Mrs. Ramirez walked up the stairs and saw Jonathan knocking. "The hospital call her to come," she told him.

"She sounded upset."

Mrs. Ramirez shook her ahead. "Poor Juana, all she does is worry. All the time at the hospital."

"What exactly is wrong with her husband?"

Mrs. Ramirez looked at Jonathan in confusion.

"No, *es* Lupe. She's the one. Don't you know? Oh, *Dios mío*. She has cancer—she dying."

"*Lupe!* What are you talking about?"

The Saldanas's door suddenly opened. Lupe's grandfather stood there, leaning on a cane.

"Where's Lupe?" Jonathan asked.

Raul paused. "She in hospital."

"She isn't really sick . . . ?"

"Yes, cancer."

Jonathan shook his head in disbelief. "But how could that *be?* How can she be sick? She's always dancing, singing, laughing?"

"Because she *believes* she fine. That's why she always talking about *quinceañera* and working for you."

"What do the doctors say?" Jonathan asked.

"One say right in front of her that she be lucky to live to 14. But she no believe it. She said she have a picture in her head that she grow up to be a lady."

"But why is she at the hospital now?"

"She has a test. Didn't she tell you?"

Jonathan looked ill. "She told me, all right. I just didn't listen."

"It's to see how bad the cancer is. They say test very painful."

Jonathan was clearly shaken. "Is there anything I can do, Mr. Saldana? Anything at all?"

"Just believe, Mr. Jonathan. That's what Lupe would say. *Believe.*"

◇ ◇

In a hospital room, Lupe, in a gown, lay on her side on a table. A doctor with a needle stood behind her.

The doctor said, "Okay, Lupe, this is the spinal tap test I told you about. It might hurt, but it will only be for a second. Are you ready?"

"Yes." Lupe's voice was brave, but her face was filled with terror. She gripped the side of the table as the doctor inserted the needle.

She caught a glimpse of herself in the chrome of a medical cart and looked into her own eyes.

She chanted softly, *"I am a beloved child of the universe, and the universe lovingly takes care of me now and forever more."* She hesitated and then added, *"I'm the belle of the ball. I'm the belle of the ball."*

◇　◇

Jonathan clumsily put away his groceries, swearing under his breath, a terrible look on his face. Eventually, the look turned to rage. He began to slam the kitchen cabinets so hard that a loose shelf behind him shook and then broke completely from the wall. A sugar jar fell and smashed onto the kitchen floor.

"Shit!" he said, as he knelt down and felt what had happened.

He was about to say more but stopped. In a hushed voice, he began to sing Lupe's swearing song. He felt his body crumble in sadness and shame.

Down on the floor, he touched the spilled sugar with his hands. Suddenly his face relaxed, and his hands began to work automatically. The window darkened as he continued.

Outside the door, he heard someone walk by.

"Who's there?"

"Mr. A. Are you okay, Mr. Jonathan?"

"Would you come here, please?"

The landlord walked in with a worried look when he saw Jonathan down on the floor.

"Are you sure you're okay?"

"Would you look at something for me?"

The landlord approached.

"You knocked over the sugar—I'll help you."

"No! I don't want it swept up. Just look at it. Does it look like anything?"

The landlord stepped back and looked at the sugar design on the floor. "It looks like a girl's face . . ." He hesitated and looked at Jonathan with a kind of wonder. "It looks like Lupe's face. That's uncanny."

Jonathan lowered his head. "Thank you."

✧　✧

After the landlord left, Jonathan got on the phone.

"I want a ten-pound bag of sand," he said into the receiver. "Delivered immediately. I'll pay whatever it is. I don't care!"

He hung up and moved into the bedroom, where he began pulling out paints, canvas, bowls, and brushes from the closet.

The deliveryman arrived to find a frantic Jonathan.

"Don't say a word! I'm blind, and I'm nuts, but I have a lot of money. Come in!"

The deliveryman carried in the sand and looked around. Jonathan had laid a canvas on the floor and arranged several bowls in a line. He was in a frenzy. He asked the deliveryman to help him mix paint and sand.

"They have to be in an order I can remember, so in the first bowl I want you to put red."

They worked for nearly an hour, mixing paint in every bowl.

When all the bowls had paint in them with various amounts of sand, Jonathan said, "There's $40 on the dresser. Take it. And thanks."

Jonathan took a knife and scooped some of the mixture onto the canvas. He spread the paint with the knife, using his other hand to feel where the paint was going.

After an hour of this, Jonathan was covered in sweat and paint. Exhausted, he lifted the canvas upright. He took a few steps back. He couldn't see what he had painted, but still he felt satisfied.

It was, he hoped, a painting of Lupe in her *quinceañera* dress.

EPILOGUE

An autumn day, three years later.

Jonathan sat at a crowded banquet table at a large party under a banner that read CONGRATULATIONS ON YOUR QUINCEAÑERA, LUPE!

A Latin band played festive music, and nearly everyone was dancing.

At one table sat Brie with a number of Lupe's classmates; another table was filled with family members, including Lupe's parents, recently returned from Mexico after Jonathan helped them find work as caretakers at a local farm. Another table had apartment dwellers and another was filled with nurses and doctors.

When the music ended, Lupe's grandfather wheeled himself to the microphone and spoke in Spanish. Beside him, his wife translated.

"Not everyone thought our darling Lupe would make it to this great day, but *we* believed, and most important, *Lupe* believed. She taught us all how to live with hope and faith and great spirit. She is our angel on earth. We all love her and thank God that she has blessed our lives."

Everyone applauded, Jonathan the loudest and longest of all.

Lupe, now 15, stood, dressed in an ornate dress, looking like a princess, her hair coiled in braids around her head. During the ensuing years, she'd grown nearly a foot; and her face had become more serene and beautiful. She smiled and placed her hands over her heart as they continued to clap for her.

She walked over to her grandparents and put her arms around their shoulders and hugged them tightly; then she turned to her parents, who were glowing with pride. Then she walked over to the table where Jonathan sat. There was a mixture of guests here: Leo, the fabric purveyor, in a brocade vest; William, the driver; Jonathan's sister, Carla, and her son, Rodney; the landlord, Mr. Antunucci; and the local deliveryman.

Jonathan's hair had grayed more at the temples, and his face was creased and lined, but there was a new aspect to his expression, a look of peace. He seemed surprised when Lupe tapped him on the shoulder.

He reached back his hand, and she took it. "Can I have this dance, please?" she asked.

When he made a courtly bow in response, she guided him out to the dance floor.

The two of them began to dance as a slow, sweet melody played.

Lupe circled Jonathan, and they moved easily, as if they had been doing this all their lives.

Jonathan whispered a few words into Lupe's ear, and she smiled up at him.

"You're welcome," she said.

As the music ended, Jonathan joyfully threw an arm in the air, and for a moment he became the living embodiment of *The Dancing Vagabond.*

About the Authors

Louise L. Hay, the author of the international bestseller *You Can Heal Your Life,* is a metaphysical lecturer and teacher with more than 50 million books sold worldwide.

For more than 30 years, Louise has helped people throughout the world discover and implement the full potential of their own creative powers for personal growth and self-healing. Louise is the founder and chairman of Hay House, Inc., which disseminates books, CDs, DVDs, and other products that contribute to the healing of the planet. Visit: www.LouiseHay.com

Lynn Lauber is a fiction and nonfiction author, teacher, and book collaborator. She has published three books of her own with W.W. Norton & Co., as well as many collaborations with other authors. Her specialties include fiction, personal narrative, and self-improvement. Her essays have appeared in *The New York Times.* She has abridged audiobooks for such authors as John Updike, Oliver Sacks, Oprah Winfrey, and Gore Vidal. Visit: www.lynnlauber.com

HAY HOUSE FILMS

Presents

The *Tales of Everyday Magic* Series

Buy the Feature Film
Painting the Future
DVD with Bonus Material • $14.95

Purchase at: www.hayhouse.com

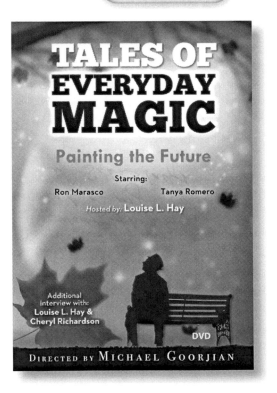

ALSO AVAILABLE

My Greatest Teacher
DVD with Bonus Material • $14.95

Purchase at: www.hayhouse.com

Based on the true life story of best-selling author Dr. Wayne W. Dyer, *My Greatest Teacher* is a compelling drama that explores the transformational power of *forgiveness*.

Dr. Ryan Kilgore is a college professor struggling to take his career to his desired level of success, while battling the very demons that are keeping him from achieving it. Kilgore is tormented by the memories of his father's abandonment, yet his wife and child are the ones who pay the price. Upon losing his grandmother, Kilgore desperately seeks the closure that he needed so long ago as he puts his future in jeopardy for a journey into the past. Through a series of mysterious and serendipitous events, a path opens that leads Kilgore to his father—and to making the choice to rebuild everything he has destroyed as a result of what had been destroying him.

Entanglement
DVD with Bonus Material • $14.95

Purchase at: www.hayhouse.com

Based on the writings of best-selling author and visionary scientist Gregg Braden, *Entanglement* explores the possibility of quantum entanglement and our connection to "the Divine Matrix."

When a daunting premonition takes U.S. art student Jack Franklin hostage, he is consumed by the thought of the danger his twin brother, Charlie, may be in. Separated by the war in Afghanistan and the constraints of modern-day technology, Jack defies the laws of science when he taps into the unexplainable physics of the Divine Matrix to try to save the life of his brother, as well as the lives of others serving with him.

The Magic Hand of Chance
DVD with Bonus Material • $14.95

Purchase at: **www.hayhouse.com**

Based on the common underlying theme of the writings of Louise L. Hay and Dr. Wayne W. Dyer—the notion that if you change your thoughts, you can change your life—this film beautifully illustrates the magical power of belief.

Filmed in Vienna against the backdrop of a traveling Russian circus, *The Magic Hand of Chance* is the true story of a clumsy magician whose life is turned around when two clowns trick him into thinking he has received the highest honor by a fictitious Magicians Society in America. Because he starts to *believe* he is great . . . he ultimately *becomes* great.

Order Your Copy Today!
DVDs Available Exclusively at
www.hayhouse.com

www.hayhouse.com®

HEAL YOUR LIFE♥
www.healyourlife.com®

www.hayhouseradio.com®

VISIONS

Hay House, Inc., P.O. Box 5100, Carlsbad, CA 92018-5100
(760) 431-7695 or (800) 654-5126
(760) 431-6948 (fax) or (800) 650-5115 (fax)
www.hayhouse.com® • **www.hayfoundation.org**

We hope you enjoyed this Hay House book. Sign up for our exclusive
free e-newsletter featuring special offers, contests, behind-the-scenes
author interviews, movie trailers, and even more bonus content, with
the latest information on exciting new Hay House products.

Sign up at:  www.hayhouse.com

Also Visit www.HealYourLife.com
The destination website for inspiration, affirmations, wisdom, success,
and abundance. Find exclusive book reviews, captivating video clips,
live streaming radio, and much more!

 HEAL YOUR LIFE♥

www.hayhouse.com®   www.healyourlife.com®   www.hayhouseradio.com®

25ᵗʰ ❂ HAY HOUSE Anniversary

Published and distributed in Australia by: Hay House Australia Pty. Ltd.,
18/36 Ralph St., Alexandria NSW 2015 • *Phone:* 612-9669-4299
Fax: 612-9669-4144 • www.hayhouse.com.au

Published and distributed in the United Kingdom by: Hay House UK, Ltd.,
292B Kensal Rd., London W10 5BE • *Phone:* 44-20-8962-1230
Fax: 44-20-8962-1239 • www.hayhouse.co.uk

Published and distributed in the Republic of South Africa by:
Hay House SA (Pty), Ltd., P.O. Box 990, Witkoppen 2068
Phone/Fax: 27-11-467-8904 • www.hayhouse.co.za

Published in India by: Hay House Publishers India,
Muskaan Complex, Plot No. 3, B-2, Vasant Kunj, New Delhi 110 070
Phone: 91-11-4176-1620 • *Fax:* 91-11-4176-1630 • www.hayhouse.co.in

Distributed in Canada by: Raincoast, 9050 Shaughnessy St.,
Vancouver, B.C. V6P 6E5 • *Phone:* (604) 323-7100
Fax: (604) 323-2600 • www.raincoast.com

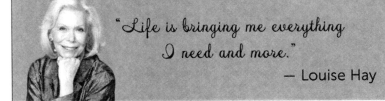

CPSIA information can be obtained at www.ICGtesting.com
Printed in the USA
BVOW071433010512

PP4530400001B/1/P